Ranger's Blood

The Rescue Rangers Book 4

Caitlyn Lynch

Shenanigans Press

Contents

Chapter 1

The phone shrilling a few inches away from his face woke Pascal Montoya from a deep, exhausted sleep. Without opening his eyes, he reached out and grabbed it, bringing it to his ear.

“What?” he growled.

“Operation Spinifex is active,” a calm female voice said on the other end of the line. “Deputy Director Spires requires you in her office immediately.”

Pascal’s eyes had snapped open after the first two words. “I’ll be half an hour. I’m at home,” he muttered, pushing himself upright.

“The Deputy Director has sent a car for you.”

"Of course she has." He ended the call and threw the phone down on the mattress, rubbing at his eyes and yawning before getting to his feet, slower than he'd like.

"Middle age catching up with me," he mumbled as he headed for the bathroom. "Or maybe it's just that I only had two hours sleep."

Thirty minutes later, though, he was getting out of the car at Langley, swiping his access card at the first of several doors and heading for his boss's office. Deputy Director of Operations Amanda Spires was sitting at her desk, immaculately attired in a midnight-blue silk skirt suit, fully made up despite it being almost three in the morning.

"Glad you could join me, Montoya," Spires murmured without looking up from the screen in front of her. "I'll be right with you."

He took a seat to wait, leaning back in the comfortable office chair and looking around. Despite her exalted rank in the Agency, Spires didn't have a fancy corner office with a view of the lawns, but a windowless cube deep in the bowels of the building. One with an open-door policy for the agents she sent out into the field to do Uncle Sam's dirty work.

"Thanks for waiting." Spires popped out an earbud and dropped it into her desk drawer. "Sorry to drag you here in the middle of the night, especially since you only just got back from Durban, but it can't wait."

"Your aide said Spinifex is active?"

"Correct." Spires' smile was tight. "We've been tracking the chatter for months, verifying the information. To the best of our ability, we have. Fortuna really does have a suitcase nuke... and he's preparing to sell it to the highest bidder."

Pascal's mouth tightened too. He'd been chasing an acquaintance with the elusive arms dealer known as Baz Fortuna for years, not just months. Ever since the CIA set up his cover identity as a broker himself.

"When's the auction going down? On the Dark Web, I presume?"

"Yes, and no. He's auctioning off places at the bidding table on the Dark Web, but the actual auction will occur at a location yet to be disclosed."

"You have to get me in."

"Teach your grandmother to suck eggs, Montoya." The DDO smirked. "We got wind of it a little late. There's one place left... and the auction closes in ten minutes. Come with me." Rising from her chair, she gestured for him to follow her.

They headed for one of the nearby operations rooms, a high-tech enclave full even at this time of night, technicians working at multi-screened workstations, managing operations occurring in real time all over the globe. Spires led him over to one of her favored techs, who glanced up at them over blue-tinted half-moon lenses and nodded.

"Montoya. Ma'am."

"How's the bidding?" Spires asked.

"Rising." The tech nodded at one of his screens. "Or at least, Fortuna thinks it is. I've locked everyone else out. I'll top it out at two twenty eight, which is forty thousand higher than any of the winning bids so far. High enough to appear legit; not so high as to make us look desperate."

"Good work, Andy." Spires tapped him on the shoulder. "I got Montoya in just in case he has to verify his identity quickly to Fortuna."

"Possibly, ma'am. I got access to the information on how much the other auctions closed at, but I can't see any private communication that occurred between Fortuna and the other buyers after that."

"Do we know who they are?"

"Working on that." Andy jerked his head at a different screen to his right, where lines of code scrolled too fast for the human eye to follow. "I'm pretty sure one of them is North Korean."

"They have their own nukes," Pascal pointed out.

"Untested, and certainly not man-portable. Huge clunky things you have to fire a ICBM to use," Spires said absently. "Which is a tad obvious. They'd pay plenty for a small device they could reverse engineer, and they're not the only ones."

"They wouldn't use it?"

"Unlikely. But they're not the only potential buyers. There are terrorist groups with real deep pockets, as you well know. Rogue nation states. Arms dealers who might be acting as middlemen, hoping to sell it on again and take a cut."

A timer below the dollar amount on Andy's screen was counting down, and Pascal happened to be looking at it when the screen suddenly blipped, going dark for a couple of seconds before coming back on.

"That timer just went wrong." He pointed.

"Say what?" Andy swiveled back from the screen of code to look.

"The screen blipped off for a couple of seconds, but the timer dropped thirty seconds." Pascal pointed. "I know what I saw," when Andy turned his head and gave him a doubtful look.

"It doesn't matter anyway. That's my bid. And the final one is going in now," Andy noted, as the timer counted down to fifteen seconds and the dollar amount changed.

"And… there we go." The timer flashed 0:00:00 and Andy raised his hand, obviously expecting a high-five. "We're the winners!"

"Andy!" Spires pointed at the screen, where the dollar amount had just changed again, jumping another twenty thousand dollars. "What the hell is that?"

"Shit!" Andy scrabbled at his keyboard, typing frantically. "Shit, shit, shit…"

"We've been outbid. Haven't we?" Pascal said after a couple of minutes as Andy typed and cursed.

"Christ almighty," Spires muttered, putting a hand to her forehead. "This is a fucking disaster. Who?"

"I'll find out. I swear I will… just give me a few minutes, ma'am…"

"My office." Spires jerked her head at Pascal, and he followed her in stunned silence.

"We have to get into that auction. We don't even know where it's taking place." Spires obviously couldn't be still, pacing around her office. "We've tried everything to intercept Fortuna and that damned nuke and got nowhere. I don't understand what happened..."

"Seems pretty obvious." Pascal sat down and folded his arms. "Somebody's a better hacker than Andy."

"A better hacker, with better computer resources, and the money backing, to beat out the Agency?" Spires gave him a disbelieving look, then halted her pacing, arrested. "Wait. Fuck."

"You're thinking it's another government agency. Mossad, or MI6 maybe?" Pascal guessed.

"It almost has to be, doesn't it? Yes, Andy?" Spires nodded for the sheepish-looking tech to enter. "It's another agency, isn't it?"

"I almost wish I could tell you it was, ma'am. It'd be less embarrassing to have been gazumped by a fellow professional."

"Then who?"

"An American private company, ma'am. Hestia Global Security."

Spires stilled. An expression Pascal couldn't quite interpret flitted across her face.

"I've not heard of them, ma'am. Do you want me to keep digging?" Andy asked, obviously keen to make up for his mistake.

"No. I've got it from here. You work on finding the other auction bidders. We need to know who we're up against." Spires dismissed him with a nod, then closed her office door, something Pascal had seen her do only rarely in his five years working for her.

"You do know who Hestia are," he assessed.

"I do." Spires started pacing again, before apparently coming to a decision and nodding sharply. Picking up the phone on her desk, she tapped a button. "Get a jet ready to go," she barked to the aide who answered the summons. "Hope you packed a go bag, Montoya."

"Always," Pascal said dryly. "Where exactly is it that we're going?"

"California." Spires bared her teeth in a parody of a smile. "Los Angeles, to be exact."

It was almost noon by the time Pascal and Spires got out of a car in the parking lot of a smallish office building in the middle of a nondescript business park in southwest Anaheim.

"This is the place?" Pascal shaded his eyes against the hot California sun and peered up at the side of the building. "It doesn't even have a name on it."

"And on Google Maps it's listed as a telephone call center." Spires slammed the car door and strode across the car park, her heeled boots clicking loudly, briefcase swinging from her hand. "This is the place."

The Deputy Director had been singularly unforthcoming during the trip, and Pascal knew her well enough not to press. A quick search on the Internet on his phone had revealed nothing: Hestia Global Security apparently didn't exist anywhere. Not on any business register or online directory.

How did a business get clients when potential customers couldn't even find them?

There was only one answer to that which made any sense. Hestia didn't need any more clients, because they already had all the work they could handle. From the government.

Which meant Hestia were either an offshoot of the government themselves - some black-funded project - or they were employed to handle jobs which the government couldn't be involved in. Jobs which required a certain degree of separation from official policy.

Plausible deniability, in other words.

Glass doors slid open at their approach, to reveal a small, apparently unmanned lobby. The only doors in sight were a pair of stainless steel elevator doors opposite them.

There was no call button.

"Uh. How do we..." Pascal started, but the elevator doors opened at that moment, to reveal a young woman.

He wasn't quite sure what he'd expected, but it wasn't long, aqua-turquoise mermaid hair rippling loose almost to her waist and a boho-style purple dress with tiny bells embroidered around the hem of the skirt tinkling at her knees, and white cowboy boots.

Pascal's gaze traveled incredulously from the hair to the boots and back again.

"Deputy Director Spires," the young woman said, smiling. "What an honor. And..?" she glanced at Pascal.

"Agent Pascal Montoya," Spires said. "We're here to speak with your Technical Director."

"And do you have an appointment?" The blue-haired woman laughed, as if in on her own joke. "Just kidding, Deputy Director. This way, if you would?"

They didn't have much choice but to follow her into the elevator. The receptionist - at least, that was what Pascal assumed she was - leaned towards a small black square on the elevator wall. A retinal scanner, he realized, as a green line of light scanned briefly down her face before the doors closed and the elevator began to move.

"How do you call the elevator?" he asked. "I didn't see a retinal scanner on the outside."

"Smart tech." She held up her wrist to show a digital watch. "This'll get you in... but you need the retinal scan to go any further."

The elevator stopped and the doors slid open again, disgorging them into a bland corridor with doors leading off either side. Further along, two men stood outside one room having a brief conversation; they looked around, saw the group entering from the elevator, and went into the office immediately, closing the door behind them.

"I know him," Pascal breathed, wracking his memory. He'd seen the taller of the two men before, and it only took a few seconds for the answer to come to him. "That was Drew Murphy. What would a tech security business want with him?"

He was speaking very softly, and the receptionist, walking ahead of them, shouldn't be able to hear. Spires leaned closer.

"Who is he?" she whispered.

"An elite sniper. One of the Rangers' best."

Pascal had been a Ranger himself before the CIA recruited him. He'd not known Murphy well, but Pascal never, ever forgot a face. Which was part of why he'd been recruited, of course.

"Interesting," was all Spires had time to say before the receptionist opened an office door - without knocking first, Pascal noticed - and gestured for them to enter.

The office inside looked more like a smaller version of the tech command center they'd left at Langley only a few hours ago rather than one person's workspace, but there was only a single office chair at the center of a horseshoe of desks, a dozen monitors hanging suspended above them, several keyboards and input devices lying on the desks.

The office chair was empty, and he and Spires shared a glance as the receptionist closed the door, remaining inside the room with them.

"Ah, the Technical Director?" Spires asked politely.

"Yes? Oh, I do beg your pardon. I didn't introduce myself. Jessikah Hagerty." She offered her hand to Spires to shake.

Pascal knew his mouth must have dropped open, and Spires showed just as much astonishment.

"*You're* the Technical Director?" Spires exclaimed. "But you're..."

"Too young? I hear that one a lot. I'm twenty-seven. But I graduated from Berkeley with a master's in computer science at eighteen and spent five years with the NSA before being headhunted for this role." Jessikah flashed a wicked little smile, perching a hip on a corner of one of the desks. "Plus, you know I'm good enough. I hacked your techs out of that auction, didn't I?"

Chapter 2

Deputy Director Spires recovered her composure with admirable speed - there were good reasons why she'd been promoted to upper management in the CIA, Jess supposed - but the agent with her was still gaping like a landed fish. There was something oddly familiar about his face. Jess studied him for a brief moment, before compartmentalizing the identification to consider later. His name wasn't pinging any bells.

"Can I offer you a seat?" She gestured to the small seating area near the single window in her office - too much light interfered with her screens, and she kept the blinds closed. "Coffee? You must have left DC very early."

"After being up all night with that auction," Spires said dryly, going over to the chairs and taking one. "Coffee would be lovely. Thank you."

"I'll get it brought in." Jess reached for one of her keyboards, typed a quick message. "Agent Montoya?"

He hadn't moved, was still standing staring at her, though he had at least closed his mouth now. She gestured. "Take a seat?"

Montoya moved, but slowly, still eyeing her. He was a big man, broad-shouldered, his suit well-tailored and not squeezing him around the shoulders as suits did on a lot of big guys. He had black hair and light brown skin, a slightly beaky nose, his eyes a light whisky-gold, piercing in their intensity. Stubble shadowed a chiseled jaw and a fan of fine lines around those golden eyes told her that he might be a little older than the early thirties she'd first guessed at.

"What is this place?" Montoya said sharply, not taking the seat. "Computer stuff, I get... but active operations?"

"Why do you say that?" She folded her arms and looked at him curiously.

"Because I recognized one of those guys in the hall when we came out of the elevator. Drew Murphy."

Jess felt her whole body still. "How do you know Drew?"

"I used to be a Ranger. Drew might not remember me, but I remember him. He's an elite sniper - a professionally sanctioned assassin, in less polite terms. And I'd very much like to know what a man like that is doing working for a *private security firm*."

Jess sniffed. Walked past him and took a seat herself, smiling at Spires. "You can ask Drew yourself, if you like. He'll tell you all about the accident which half-blinded him, invalided him out of the Rangers. A slightly complicated path led him to us, but he's a valued member of our team. And let's be clear about it; none of the alphabet agencies would have taken him on because of his *disability*." She nearly spat the last word, still angry about it. "He can't hit a dime at a quarter mile any more, but he's certainly not useless, and we're certainly not using him as any sort of assassin!"

There was a brief silence, and then Montoya sat down, inclining his head slightly to her. "I apologize. I didn't know Murphy had been in an accident."

"And that's all you're apologizing for?" Jess blinked.

"If we could talk about the issue at hand?" the deputy director interrupted before Jess could rip the judgy agent a new asshole. "Your interference in one of our operations."

"Is this where you threaten to arrest me because I'm a national security threat?" Amused and entirely unafraid, Jess leaned back in her chair and crossed her legs.

"No, it's where you tell us who's bankrolling your operation and then I go to my counterpart at that agency and have them hand it back to us." Spires crossed her legs too and smiled.

Jess thought about it. Thought about possible repercussions. Figured that Spires was going to find out anyway, one way or another. "Homeland Security," she said finally.

"Of course." Spires shared a glance with Montoya, nodded. "Thank you for your cooperation, Ms. Hagerty."

"Wait, that's it? You personally flew all the way here just to ask me that?" Startled, Jess sat up straight.

"I figured I couldn't send just anyone. They wouldn't get in the door. Would they?"

"Well, no."

"I've no doubt you knew we were onto you last night. Probably the moment my tech came to me with Hestia's name. Quite possibly, you allowed him to find it."

Jess's respect for the deputy director went up several notches. "Yes, ma'am," she admitted.

"You didn't want to be fending us off until the auction went down," Montoya murmured, and she nodded tightly.

"To be honest, yes. You're welcome to fight it out at whatever levels in Washington you operate on, Deputy Director. I don't want any part of that." She hesitated. "But in all fairness. I need to tell you that you don't have much time. I have 24 hours from the time the auction closed to provide further credentials to Fortuna, and then 48 hours from then to get to a location he has yet to designate, for the auction."

"Shit." Spires' mouth twisted, and Jess understood. The wheels in Washington ground pretty slow. The last thing Spires needed was some inter-agency bickering about who had jurisdiction and was running the operation.

"So I have to request that you bow out gracefully and leave us to handle things," Jess said, more in hope than optimism. The CIA weren't known for bowing out gracefully, in her experience.

Spires looked thoughtful, tapping her fingertip against her lip. "Who are you sending in? Not you, presumably." She gave a scornful little laugh. "Unless you've also managed to develop a reputation as an international arms dealer I don't know about. Your resumé is impressive, but..."

"Not that impressive." Jess took a deep breath, telling herself she dealt with people assuming she wasn't competent because of her age all the time. Although the truth was, it happened a lot less often than it used to, because she mostly interacted with people via her keyboard these days. "One of my colleagues will play the part of a disaffected politician with dark money backing..."

Spires was already shaking her head. "It won't work. Fortuna is extremely suspicious. Your man won't even make it to the auction. You need someone whose reputation will pass scrutiny." Her smile was shark-like. "Someone like Pascal."

"I'm sorry, how exactly does a CIA agent manage to pass the scrutiny of Baz Fortuna?" Jess scoffed, but the part of her brain she'd tasked with recalling where she knew Montoya's face from was finally dredging the memory to the surface.

"Pascal is deep undercover, and has been ever since joining the Agency. As..."

"Pascal Montalban." Suddenly, she put it together. "That's where I know your face. You're on a ton of watch lists. A French-Algerian broker to the world's most wanted warlords."

He tipped his head, smirking slightly. "Very good."

"I ran you through the wrong facial recognition databases," she murmured, disappointed in herself. "I assumed you were legit."

"I am legit!" Pascal looked annoyed.

"Know Baz Fortuna personally, do you?"

"Not yet. But I will. Once you hand back control of the operation to us."

Jess chewed on her lip, looking from one to the other of the CIA agents. She had to admit that Pascal Montalban would have a much greater chance of making it to Fortuna's inner sanctum than Hestia's original plan.

She just didn't like giving up control of what she'd worked so hard to obtain, and she knew Homeland Security would be displeased she'd let CIA waltz in and take over without a fight.

"What about a joint operation?" she suggested.

Spires looked amused, made a dismissive little sound. Pascal, though, tilted his head and seemed to examine her again.

"Go on," he said slowly. "Pitch it to me."

"I've demonstrated my tech skills already. Fact is, by the time you've flown back to DC and I've handed over to your *inferior* tech people, the 24 hours will be just about up and then you've got to move fast to make the meet, wherever it is. Stay here and we'll run the initial contact from here. Verify your bona fides. I'll continue to provide whatever tech support you need throughout the operation. In concert with your people, if you insist. And if it turns out the weapon or Baz Fortuna are on US soil, you let Homeland handle the action. They'll be happy with that." She didn't think it all that likely - Fortuna was too canny an operator to let himself be caught on US soil - but as long as the problem was handled, Homeland wouldn't complain.

Montoya looked at Spires. "I think we should take her up on it."

Spires stared at him. “Montoya, are you mad? She’s…”

“Competent.”

Startled, Jess blinked and stared at him. “Did you just pay me a compliment?”

“You said it yourself. You’ve demonstrated your capabilities. Seriously, ma’am,” he addressed Spires, “can you name another hacker who could have hacked Andy out of a situation he had under full control? With such precise timing? Can you even tell me where we should go about looking for such a person?”

Spires was tapping her fingernail against her lip again. “No,” she admitted finally, looking Jessikah over before looking back at Montoya. “You’re not wrong about her abilities, but you’d be putting your life in her hands. It’s your call.”

“Then I say we go for it.”

It wasn’t the outcome she’d expected from this meeting, but Jess wasn’t about to complain. She offered her hand to Montoya, who shook it, strong fingers curling around hers and grasping firmly. For an instant she thought he was going for a crusher grip, but he released her before the squeeze.

Her watch chirped discreetly, and Jess rose to her feet, going over to the door. "That'll be the coffee. Come on in. Oh... Liane."

It was her sister Liane who brought the coffee in. A highly trained former ATF agent who'd spent almost her entire career undercover, she was the one who'd been intended to go in as the prospective buyer for the nuke. Liane had volunteered, and she was certainly capable, but considering what Spires had said, Jess was quietly glad Liane wouldn't have to go.

"Would you ask Drew to come in?" Jess asked quietly as she took the tray from Liane's hands.

"Sure." Liane gave her interrogative eyebrows.

"Turns out the guy's a former Ranger. He recognized Drew."

"Huh." Liane nodded, though, turning to leave.

“And then come back yourself. Change of plan on Fortuna. It won’t be you going in.”

“Can’t say I’m sorry,” Liane admitted with a quick grin. She slipped back out and Jess turned back towards the seats. Montoya stood gallantly to take the tray and ease it down to the table, and she murmured thanks.

Liane had put not only a coffee pot with milk, sugar and cups on the tray, but also a plate with several brownies on it. Jess eyed them hungrily. She’d not had a lot of sleep after the excitement of the early-morning auction, and breakfast hadn’t happened yet.

“Please do help yourselves,” she said graciously, and waited until Montoya and Spires had done so before pouring herself a large black coffee, dumping four spoons of sugar in it and grabbing a brownie.

She saw Montoya smile into his own, unsweetened black coffee. Of course. He’d probably started drinking it like that in the Rangers and never stopped. Spires had added a dash of creamer, but no sugar, though she had been tempted by the brownies and was nibbling delicately at one.

The door opened again and Drew and Liane came in. Montoya put his cup down and rose with a smile; to Jess's astonishment, the expression completely transformed his face, from a rather austere grimness to a level of handsomeness that actually made her blink.

"Drew Murphy, in the flesh. Good to see you."

Drew was smiling too, stepping forward to offer his hand to shake. "Major Montoya. It's been a long time."

"*Major*," Liane mouthed to Jess, making an impressed face. They both knew a little about how difficult it was to achieve rank in the Rangers, where literally every soldier was already in the top one per cent. Drew, when he talked about the officers he'd worked under, spoke of them with great respect.

"Staff Sergeant… is that where you topped out? I always thought you could have gone officer track, myself." Montoya nodded towards Drew's scarred eye, the blue iris cloudy. "I'm sorry to hear about your injury. That must have been traumatic."

"Messed me up mentally for a while, but I found a new cause to fight for. Turns out I'm good for more than just pulling a trigger." Drew accepted the condolence gracefully. "Private sector pays a lot better too." He tipped his head meaningfully towards Spires. "Probably a lot better than even your department of the government."

Spires let out a disbelieving laugh. "Are you trying to recruit him from right under my nose?"

Drew's grin was unapologetic. "Well, Jess would have the final say... but I'd vouch for him."

They made small talk for another couple of minutes, and then Liane and Drew left again, closing the door behind them. Jess took her seat and steeled herself. There was no way Spires was going to miss the implication.

"The final say, hm?" Spires said immediately. "Why do I feel like Technical Director isn't your only title at Hestia Global Security, Ms Hagerty?"

Jess winced. "So maybe 'founding partner' would be a bit more accurate," she said, "but come on... do you blame me? Look how you reacted to my age and the way I look. I'd never be trusted to handle anything sensitive if you thought the buck stopped here."

There was a long, fraught silence, and then Montoya said, "Founding *partner*?"

She sighed, nodded. "My partner is the 'face' of the business, for senior officials in the government. He had a long and distinguished career with the Navy, then served a term in Congress. We met while I was working for the NSA, a black hat hacker stole some confidential information from his computers and I was tasked to track down the culprit and recover it. I was at the point of quitting and figuring out how to start up Hestia on my own... you could say I recruited him, really. He's a figurehead. Spends most of his time on the golf course."

"You're very honest," Spires said, tilting her head and examining Jess curiously. "I like that. And from everything I've heard about Hestia, you've never yet failed to deliver results, which I like even better. You have people like Drew Murphy and your sister working for you - you didn't introduce her, but I recognized her. Former ATF agent. Wrapped up that biker gang human trafficking ring in Idaho last year," she told Montoya, who clearly didn't have a clue what she was talking about but nodded anyway. "Is it her you planned to send in to Fortuna?"

"Yes, and to be honest, I'm glad she doesn't have to go. She's a brilliant undercover agent, but the cover we'd built for her is thinner than I'd like. Plus, as a woman she'd likely be at a different kind of disadvantage in that situation. We'd hoped to send Drew in as a bodyguard too, but there are no guarantees Fortuna would allow it. This?" Jess made a circle with her finger, indicating the three of them. "In my professional opinion, has a much greater chance of success."

"I agree," Spires said, surprising her a little. "And to be honest with you in return, Ms. Hagerty, if you weren't clearly doing very well for yourself in the private sector, I'd be desperately trying to recruit you to the Agency right about now. As it is, I believe we'll certainly be using Hestia's services in the future. Now." She clapped her hands together. "Do we have to wait 24 hours to provide these bona fides to Fortuna, or can we get started now so Montoya and I can find a hotel and get some damn sleep?"

Chapter 3

Fortuna had set up any number of virtual hoops for them to jump through, but Montoya rose to them all admirably. He had a whole set of apparently completely legitimate documents for Pascal Montalban.

"Does Montalban just broker arms?" Jess murmured, her fingers flying over keys as Montoya stood behind her, watching what she was doing.

"Anything his clients require," Montoya replied, warm breath brushing her ear.

Jess suppressed a shiver. "Must be lucrative. Does the Agency let you keep any of your commission?" she joked.

His offended silence was answer enough.

"There," she said, tapping a blunt fingernail on the Enter key. "That should be all of it."

A message came back a few seconds later.

"Ugh, not all of it! They want 30 seconds of video footage of you reading a paper edition of any newspaper published today. And we have one hour to deliver it."

"Gives no time to make a deep fake," Montoya murmured. "It has to be really me."

"No... but I don't think anyone in the building will have a *paper* edition. I'll have to send someone out for one."

"No need," Spires said, opening her briefcase. "Here's the early edition of the *Washington Post*. Will that do?"

"I s'pose," Jess said. "But do you really want a Washington paper? If I was an arms dealer that would kind of scream *undercover government agent* to me."

Spires looked struck, like that hadn't even occurred to her. Smart woman, but one who didn't get out of her little DC enclave enough, Jess guessed. She typed a quick message, asking Liane to get a newspaper ASAP.

"A San Diego Union-Tribune if we can, I think," she murmured, adding that to the request. "Should be available, and it doesn't pinpoint our location. Does Montalban have any links to San Diego?"

"Any number of deals settled there with clients on both sides of the border. Good choice," Montoya said, and Jess told herself that his approval absolutely should not be making her feel warm inside.

No. Do not start finding him attractive, she ordered herself sternly. *Bad call. Bad libido*.

Liane delivered the paper a few minutes later and they filmed a quick video of Pascal sitting in one of Jess's chairs leafing through it. The closed blinds behind him ensured nobody would be able to identify where the video was shot, and Jess was careful to strip all metadata off before uploading the file.

Within a few minutes, the response came back. A link to a new video file. Jess checked it for viruses or trackers before opening it.

"What the hell?" Spires murmured as the view panned through what looked like a hotel lobby, then skipped to a pool, several beautiful women in bikinis lying around it.

"*Wave, girls,*" a voice ordered, and the girls obediently waved to the camera.

"*You are invited,*" the voice said then, "*to a very special auction in a very special location. And this is where I tell you that the rumours you have heard are greatly un-exaggerated, because I have not one device to sell.*"

The camera view changed again, and Spires, Montoya and Jess all sucked in harsh breaths.

"*I have three.*"

"Fuck!" Spires said what they were all thinking as they stared at the screen, at the image of three hard-shelled suitcases laying open, each one containing what for all the world appeared to be a small nuclear bomb.

"*You will have three opportunities to bid for one of these devices. Be at Boquerón Airport, Puerto Rico at eleven a.m. on Wednesday morning, and be prepared to stay for a few days at my private island retreat. Do not bring any communications devices or any technology at all with you. Any attempt to circumvent this requirement will result in you not being permitted to attend the auction."* The voice, which had turned serious, became cheerful once again as the view changed from the suitcase bombs back to the women by the swimming pool. *"You may bring a companion if you wish to keep yourself amused; otherwise, my friends here will be glad to keep you company. See you soon on Isla Fortuna!"*

The screen went black as the video ended.

"Play it again," Spires demanded, and Jess clicked the link again, but the video was already gone, deleting itself from the internet. "Shit!"

"Easy," Jess lifted a placating hand. "I was recording it as we watched. I can bring it up again. But if you're looking for identifying features, I think you're going to struggle." The video had been very carefully shot, no features of landscape visible anywhere. There were some possibilities with the hotel lobby style shots, if she could find anything matching them, but they looked very generic. She'd write a program to search, but didn't hold out much hope.

"A private island," Montoya said, obviously thinking aloud. "That explains quite a lot about Fortuna. He vets potential buyers and brings them to him; he doesn't need to go to them."

"And there's nothing here that indicates the devices are actually on the island," Jess pointed out as the video played again and the suitcase bombs appeared. "They could be anywhere. My guess is that they *are* elsewhere; if Fortuna was raided, he wouldn't want anything incriminating found. Just him and his buddies enjoying vacation time in the sunshine."

"*Three* devices." Spires looked slightly sick as she made her way back to the chairs and sat down, putting her face in her hands briefly. "This is a nightmare. Three devices, three buyers... three potential incidents which could kick off a world war."

"We have to stop all of them," Montoya said, clearly thinking it through. "And with no technology permitted on Isla Fortuna - wherever it is - I can't get word back about who the other buyers and where the devices are."

"There's technology there," Jess disagreed immediately. She ran the video back, paused it at one of the lobby shots. "See that? Surveillance camera, and a pretty new one. WiFi connected. You just can't take tech with you. You'll need to appropriate some that's already there."

"What if I can't? I'm sure he has it under guard. And encrypted, too. I'll be straight with you; tech's not my strong point. I have all the basics but I wouldn't have a clue how to go about hacking something password-protected, even."

"Then I'll have to come in with you."
Jess shrugged. Inwardly, a little voice was screaming, *What are you doing??? You hate field work!* "You heard him; he said you can bring a companion. I'll come as your girlfriend."

"Absolutely not." Montoya's tone was flat.

"Now, just a minute, Pascal," Spires said. "I don't see that we have any choice."

"Of course we do! There has to be someone on CIA's payroll who can do the job."

"I don't think Andy would be convincing as your girlfriend." Spires' lips twitched at her own joke. "We don't have *time*," she went on, when he didn't laugh. "You have to be in Puerto Rico in less than two days. We'd have to get someone flown down from Langley, briefed and up to speed - and to be honest, I really can't think of anyone who's available right now who could do the job. Jess can. I don't doubt her technical skills."

Jess couldn't help but preen, just a tiny bit.

"I don't doubt her technical skills either," Montoya said, "but the other part of the role..." he gestured at Jess. "She doesn't look the part."

"Not your type, Montoya?" she needled back, offended.

"You don't look like an arms broker's arm candy," he said, quite bluntly.

"Not pretty enough?" A little hurt, she folded her arms.

"Your face is. Your figure's fine. The hair and the clothes? Disastrous."

"Say what you think, why don't you!"

“Children,” Spires said mildly. “That will do. Ms. Hagerty. Are you willing to go in with Pascal? You know the risks, I’m sure. We’ll ensure you’re well compensated... but we really do need your help. Trying to bring on another agent with the right skill set at this late stage presents some serious risks.”

“I understand. Yes. I’m prepared to go in. And Mr Montoya will just have to trust that I’m capable of presenting myself as the kind of arm candy who won’t make Fortuna even blink.” She shot him a poisonous look.

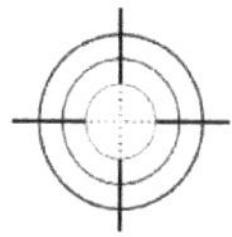

Pascal winced as Jessikah glared at him. He deserved that, he supposed. “You have documents?” he asked, as a peace offering. “Otherwise, we can provide some.”

“I have several cover identities. One of them will do. Give me your credit card.” She held out her hand.

“Excuse me?”

"What I don't have is suitable clothing, to look like a rich man's arm candy. I'll go get my hair fixed... go shopping. Least the CIA can do is pay for it."

Spires nodded, and Montoya sighed. Fished out his wallet and handed over his Agency credit card, already thinking dismally of how he was going to explain the expense report. Hopefully Spires would just sign it and save him the trouble.

"I always wanted to go shopping on Rodeo Drive." Jessikah's smile was wicked. "Now I have an excuse."

Pascal winced.

"We'll go find a hotel. Get flights booked to get you to Puerto Rico in time... from San Diego, I think. You can drive down there tomorrow evening, stay the night, get an early morning flight." Spires was looking at her phone. "Boquerón is halfway round the island from San Juan - better organize a helicopter, I think."

"I'll leave that to your resources." Jessikah rose to her feet, and they were left with no choice but to let her escort them down to the ground floor and outside. “My number.” She handed Spires a business card. “Let me know where and what time to meet tomorrow.”

The car and driver which had brought them was still waiting; Pascal was silent as they got into the back seat and Spires told the driver to take them to a hotel. Even though the driver was a fellow agent, they did not discuss the mission in the car. It was too sensitive, too critical.

“You’re going to be on your own, pretty much,” Spires said once they were in a hotel room, having quickly swept for bugs. “You can’t carry any tech, which means we daren’t even put a tracker on you. We’ll try to track you real-time using satellites, but...”

“We have to operate on the assumption that Fortuna will have thought of that and taken steps.”

“It’ll be just you and Ms. Hagerty until she’s able to find and hack some tech to get a message out to us.”

“And we can’t risk doing that too often,” Pascal pointed out. “She might only get one opportunity. If she gets caught...” he didn’t like to think about it. Fortuna might hesitate to do anything to him, knowing Pascal Montalban had powerful friends. Jessikah would have no such protection, only what Pascal himself could offer her, and he had to be careful to stay in character. The ruthless, amoral broker Montalban wouldn't care particularly for whatever woman graced his arm at any given moment, certainly wouldn't intervene if Fortuna caught her hacking his tech to pass information to the CIA!

"I think she might surprise you," Spires said. She tossed Pascal the business card Jessikah had given her. "Make your arrangements. And remember. You're supposed to be sleeping with her. I can see you don't like her much, but you'd better figure out how to make it look convincing, because Fortuna's going to notice if the pair of you are sniping at each other instead of fucking."

"I can make it look convincing," Pascal said shortly.

"See that you do." Rising to her feet, Spires headed for the door. "I'm going back to DC, you don't need me here. Keep me in the loop as long as you can. I'll be talking to the folks at Homeland, make sure we're all on the same page when it comes to the intercepts."

He nodded, unsurprised that she was leaving. He was a little surprised she'd come at all, though relieved; he had the distinct feeling he'd never have even made it in the door of Jessikah's office, never mind convinced her to work with them to make the operation happen.

"Good luck," Spires said on her way out the door. "The full might of the Agency's resources is behind you, Pascal. Use what you need."

The full might of the Agency's resources, and it was going to come down to him and a youthful, blue-haired white hat hacker, he thought as the door closed, to prevent three suitcase nukes ending up God knew where in the hands of God knew who.

Fantastic.

Just fucking fantastic.

Chapter 4

Pascal checked his phone, pulled the rental car to the curb outside a steel gate and looked through the bars with raised eyebrows.

Seemed like Jessikah Hagerty was indeed doing pretty well for herself in the private sector, if this was her house. On a cul-de-sac in the Hidden Canyon estates, he reckoned the elegant, glass-and-steel modern building would probably be a cool couple of million at least.

“I’ll be right out,” a voice crackled from the intercom before he could even reach for the button, and he smiled wryly. Of course she’d probably watched him arrive on several different cameras.

From the very small amount of information he'd been able to dredge up about her time at the NSA, she was so thorough she'd probably cloned his phone while he was in her office and had been tracking him with it ever since.

The gate slid open just enough for a large wheeled suitcase to be pushed out, and then Jessikah followed it.

Pascal wasn't a man who shocked easily, but his jaw dropped open, because she was almost unrecognizable. Gone was the blue-haired boho hippy chick of yesterday, and in her place stood a glamorous blonde in a sleeveless blazer dress and skyscraper heels, a fine gold chain belt emphasizing her tiny waist, the front unbuttoned far enough to show a glorious V of cleavage.

He gaped, dazzled.

"Do I pass muster?" She smirked at him before nudging the suitcase forward. "Are you going to make like a gentleman and put this in the car? It weighs a ton, I'm afraid. Jessica Berry-Sandford, Instagram model, doesn't travel light."

"I... right. Instagram model?"

"One of my aliases. Pretty easy to keep up. She's a rich kid who only posts pictures of herself when she feels like it; most of her shots are aesthetics... lifted from all over the internet." Donning a pair of crystal-encrusted Cartier sunglasses he seriously hoped hadn't been paid for on his credit card, she swanned around him and slipped into the passenger seat. "What a boring car. Do I take it you're still Pascal Montoya?"

Amused despite himself, he hefted the case - Louis Vuitton, what else - into the trunk and joined her. "Pascal Montalban would never be caught dead in a car like this. He likes vintage sports cars. 1960s Jaguars, for preference. But I'm not Pascal Montalban yet. He's persona non grata in the US. He won't come out until we get to Puerto Rico. For now, I'm Peter Miller, insurance agent. Going to San Juan on holiday... with the girlfriend who's way out of his league, apparently."

Jessikah's laugh rang out as he started the engine. "Y'all got that right, sugar."

Her accent was Southern and sounded utterly natural. He couldn't resist asking her about it as he drove south, and she answered freely, telling him she grew up in southern Virginia. Her parents both DC lobbyists, she and her sisters had spent a fair bit of time with their grandmother in Macon, Georgia... which was where the accent came from.

"It's my natural accent. I worked hard to lose it while I was at the NSA. People don't take you seriously."

"And you already had too much of that problem," he said.

"Exactly! And I can't communicate with everyone via only email, much though I'd like to try." She cranked her seat all the way back, tugged her shoes off and flung her feet up on the dash. "Ugh, the one thing I haven't had time to do is get used to wearing heels again."

"You shouldn't have to for long," Pascal felt the need to point out. "Can't see them being much use on Isla Fortuna, wherever it is."

"Are you kidding?" She nudged the sunglasses down her nose, peered at him over them. "Did you look closely at the girls on that video?"

He really hadn't, but didn't want to admit it.

"They were literally wearing nothing but skimpy bikinis... and high heels. Fortuna will expect nothing less. I've got six pairs of Jimmy Choos in that suitcase."

"I seriously hope they didn't go on my credit card!" He winced.

She snickered into her hand. "Relax," she said, but she didn't tell him they weren't on his card.

Traffic was light and they made the airport in plenty of time.

"Montalban doesn't fly private?" Jess needled lightly as they checked in for their flight.

"*Peter Miller* certainly doesn't," Pascal said in a warning tone. "He did splash out for business class, though. Probably to impress his high-maintenance girlfriend."

"Acceptable," she said with a little sniff. "Barely."

He could hardly believe she wasn't the Instagram model she was pretending to be. Heads turned as she stalked through the airport on those spindly heels, her hips swaying in a dangerous rhythm that men couldn't help but stare at. Golden hair rippling almost to her hips - he shuddered to think what her hair extensions would have cost - she talked and laughed a little too loud, everything exaggerated, calculated to draw the eye.

In short, she was one hell of an actress, and any doubts he'd had about her being able to fool Fortuna faded away. She wasn't precisely the kind of woman who'd been seen on Montalban's arm before - beautiful enough but she was a little too confident - but Pascal figured he could just imply he was actually a bit smitten with her.

It wouldn't be difficult.

He would really rather not be attracted to Jessikah. She was over a decade his junior and he was responsible for her safety on one of the most complicated and dangerous missions he'd ever been on, but he'd always had a weakness for clever, opinionated women. She was sharp as a whip, absolutely beautiful in both incarnations he'd seen thus far, and apparently fearless.

"You said you left NSA four years ago?" he asked, when they were sitting in a quiet corner of the business-class lounge.

"I didn't say that precisely, no, but it's certainly information you could have gotten when you went digging." The corners of her mouth curled up in that little smirk again.

"Hm. I'm sure NSA had physical requirements for their agents. What I want to know is have you kept up with the training since you left?"

"Ah." She tilted her head slightly. "You're wondering if you're going to have to carry me if the shooting starts."

"I seriously hope it won't start and you won't need to do a thing, but humor me. We've no time for me to do an assessment of your skills, so I need you to be honest with me." He fixed her with a direct stare.

"Fair enough." Jess sat back, crossing her long legs at the knee.

He forced himself not to look down, to maintain eye contact. *Don't get distracted.*

"Since you asked for honesty, I admit I'd let myself slack off a bit physically since leaving the NSA and starting Hestia. When my sister came in to join us last year, though, she pretty much grabbed me by the collar and took me back to the gym, and the firing range too. I'm sure I'm not up to whatever black belt ninja standards the Agency might demand of its field agents, but I'll hold my own."

Her blue eyes were unwavering, and he nodded slowly, believing her. "Your sister has quite the reputation. ATF were very sorry to lose her." He'd read up on Liane Hagerty as well, finding her file to be quite a bit thicker than Jessikah's. It was impressive reading.

"Then they shouldn't have treated her like crap. They kept her undercover too long and she was just about burned out after that business with the Brethren. A year running a roadhouse in the back end of nowhere, Idaho... I don't know how she stuck it so long."

"Undercover work takes a lot of patience." He thought of the five years he'd put in, patiently building Pascal Montalban's cover. Doing some things which put stains on his soul, but had been sanctioned by the Agency for the sake of the larger mission.

"You'd know, huh?" Jess smiled again, more sympathetic than the smirk. "I get that you're the lead on this," she said, leaning forward suddenly and touching his knee lightly, surprising him. "I'm not going to undercut you or do anything silly or reckless. I'm along because you need tech support, which is a role I'm very used to playing, believe me. The bimbo girlfriend thing... I'll do my best."

"You'll do great." He meant it. She looked and sounded the part. "Just one thing. Remember to make a hell of a fuss when I tell you to hand over your phone."

"An Instagram model would be nearly as attached to her phone as I am." Jessikah laughed quietly. "I'll remember to whine about it once we're on the island, too."

A businessman came over to join them in their corner of the lounge, staring blatantly at Jessikah's legs. She gave him a coy little smile and preened, the very image of an Instagram model enjoying the admiration which was her just due.

Their flight was called at that moment and Jess rose gracefully to her feet, favoring the dazzled businessman with a smile before swaying off towards the gate. There was nothing else Pascal could do but follow in her wake.

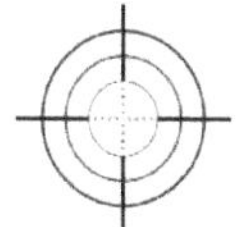

The flight was uneventful and they were ensconced in an upmarket hotel on the outskirts of San Juan just before midnight. Pascal had reserved a two-bedroom suite, aware this was the last night of privacy Jessikah was going to get for the next little while. They still needed to talk about what they might expect once they reached Isla Fortuna, and he ordered a room service dinner while Jess took a shower, steeling himself for the conversation.

“Smells good.” Jess stepped back into the room, wrapped in a terry toweling robe. “That meal on the plane didn’t fill much of a hole, despite being business class level catering.”

"You had the beef, so I concluded you weren't vegetarian." He lifted the steel dome off a plate to reveal a perfectly done steak, with French fries and a side salad.

"Oh my God, yum." She almost threw herself into a chair and grabbed up her knife and fork. "I'm starved."

"What would you like to drink?" He opened the minibar to inspect the selection.

"Beer," Jess said around her first mouthful of steak.

"Gotcha." He cracked a bottle, set it down in front of her. "Um… you're aware that…"

"On Isla Fortuna, I must eat and drink like an Instagram model. Uh huh." She toasted him with her beer. "But we're in San Juan, so as far as I'm concerned, what happens in San Juan stays in San Juan.

"Right." Taking his own seat, he applied himself to his meal, waiting for the right moment to bring up what he needed to talk about.

Once again, Jessikah surprised him.

“So,” she said, between bites, “we should talk about the intimacy thing.”

“Uh?” Pascal said intelligently, caught off guard.

“Because we have to look like we’re comfortably intimate with each other, and so far it’s not going well. You nearly jumped out of your skin when I touched your knee earlier.”

He fought the instinctive reaction to deny that he’d jumped, because she was correct. He had. He’d reacted to her touch because the attraction he felt for her was so strong, too strong. He couldn’t not react.

And he had to, somehow, get on top of it. Make it look like he was both comfortable with her and secure in her affections. Completely accustomed to touching her… and felt entitled to do so at his whim, because that’s how Pascal Montalban would treat a woman.

“I was trying to give you space for as long as possible,” he said finally, “because you have to understand I won’t be treating you with any respect for the next few days.”

"I figured." She sat back, nursing her beer. "Tell me about Pascal Montalban. I need to understand who he is."

"I thought you knew all about him," he sniped gently.

"Ha. I have no doubt you control very carefully any tiny snippet of information that's out there about him. About all I know about him apart from some information on the deals he's brokered is that he's supposedly French-Algerian." She tilted her head to one side, inspecting him. "Which you do fit, facially. Close to the truth?"

"As is any good cover story. My mother's French-Algerian, my father Cuban-American. Which is where the name Montoya comes from."

"That sounds like an interesting story, how two people from that background met!"

"You'll probably think it's quite romantic." He grinned, thinking of his parents. "My mom was working as a cleaner at the American Embassy in Paris. My dad was a very junior State Department employee stationed there on his first assignment. Both of them say it was love at first sight."

"That is *very* romantic! They still together?"

"Yep. They retired to France together a few years ago, live in a quiet little village in the Loire Valley. Rustic paradise." He thought of it wistfully; it had been too long since he'd been able to stop by for a visit. Maybe after this mission was done.

"So you must be bilingual - trilingual?"

"Quadrilingual natively. English, Spanish, French, and Algerian Arabic. And I have something of a gift for picking up languages," he understated.

"Ahhhh." It was a long-drawn out sound. "Suddenly it makes absolute sense the CIA snatched you up."

"Yeah, the Army tried to direct me down the Military Intelligence track because of my language skills but I had my heart set on the Rangers." He shrugged. "CIA basically waited until I showed signs of being disaffected with being shot at, and then swooped in and head-hunted me."

"To get shot at for them instead?"

"Perhaps surprisingly, it's rarely come to that. I can count on one hand the number of times a gun has even been pointed in my direction in the last five years."

"I'm guessing Pascal Montalban would react badly to anyone pointing a gun at him?"

"Let's just say things don't usually end well for anyone stupid enough to try it!"

Jessikah grinned, and then, still watching him, deliberately leaned back further in her chair, swung her legs up and put her feet in his lap. "They're sore after the heels," she prompted gently, and Pascal, who'd had to steel himself not to flinch, nodded. Carefully, he began to massage her feet, thinking how smart she was, choosing a method to ease them both into getting physically comfortable with each other that wasn't too intimate.

How he was going to cope when they had to be a lot more intimate remained to be seen.

Chapter 5

Jess ordered herself to breathe deeply as Pascal's strong fingers pressed into the balls of her feet, soothing the aching flesh. She'd teased him about reacting to her touch, but the truth was, even the slightest brush of his fingers against hers earlier had made every hair on her arm stand on end. She'd never been this hyper-aware of a man in her life and it was both disconcerting and extremely inconvenient.

It was impossible not to notice how attractive he was, with those piercing gold eyes and his sharply chiseled cheekbones, but having his full attention on her felt like being stared at by a golden eagle. Like she was prey and he was considering a snack.

The really alarming part was that she was starting to think being eaten up sounded fantastic.

“I should get some sleep,” she said, a little abruptly. “If the helicopter is picking us up at nine, I need to spend at least half an hour on hair and makeup before we leave, and it’s nearly two now.”

“Yeah.” Pascal let her feet slide from his lap, stood up. “It’s going to be a tough week. Get some rest.”

“You too,” she said quietly, turning away and heading for the room she’d claimed.

“Jessikah?”

“Yeah?” she looked back.

He gave her that intent look again, and she couldn’t help the shiver that ran up her spine.

“You’re going to do great.”

Self-belief wasn’t something Jess had ever lacked, but she had to confess, if only to herself, that she’d had a few qualms of doubt since Deputy Director Spires had told her that she needed to go in on the mission.

She'd never done undercover work in her life. Yes, she'd built aliases and maintained them, but it was an abstract exercise, something that amused her rather than something she'd thought ever might be a real necessity. Hacking government databases and social media networks was practice.

Things had suddenly got very real. She was about to walk into the den of one of the world's most wanted criminals, attempt to fool him into thinking her a brainless piece of arm candy, and hack his own tech to help the CIA gain custody of three suitcase nukes before they were dispersed to fanatics and terrorists who might use them to create unthinkable tragedy.

Hearing Pascal say she could do it, that he believed in her, might be just words, but it definitely gave her confidence a boost.

"I hope you're right," she said quietly before closing the bedroom door behind her.

If possible, Jessikah looked even more fabulous the following morning, in a blue dress which appeared to be not much more than a few triangles of fabric held together with large-ring gold chains. Smooth golden skin was visible at her sides, and Pascal wondered absently if she'd gotten a spray tan. She didn't seem like the type of woman to enjoy lying around getting a tan... frankly, he doubted she could stay still long enough.

"You look spectacular," he said quietly, picking up her suitcase. "Honestly... so spectacular I can't imagine Fortuna and his men getting their brains out of their pants long enough to consider you as any kind of threat."

"Here's hoping." She smiled up at him, then arched an eyebrow and slowly reached up to kiss his cheek. He held still, and then, just as slowly as she'd moved, curled his free arm around her waist and held her close to him. He felt Jessikah freeze for the barest instant but then she softened, melting and curving against him.

"We can do this," she whispered.

“We absolutely can, and we’re absolutely going to. No matter what it takes.” His tone was a warning; she nodded in silent understanding.

“No matter what.”

The helicopter was waiting for them, and as they walked up, Pascal consciously put on the mantle of Pascal Montalban, broker of shady deals for the world’s most undesirable tyrants and terrorists. He added a little swagger to his walk, a sneering curl to his lip. A French accent to his tone when he said;

“Good. You’re on time.”

“Of course, sir.” The pilot was one he’d used before, knew who he was and showed suitable deference. The man shot one slightly dazzled look at Jess before averting his eyes and picking up her suitcase to load into the chopper’s cargo bay.

“You have the lockbox?” Pascal asked as they got into the helicopter and he made a show of helping Jessikah put on her safety harness.

“Yes, sir, and it’ll be held in our office safe until you request its return.” The pilot handed him an open metal box. “You can set the combination yourself, as you requested.”

He did that as they took the short flight from San Juan to Boquerón, on Puerto Rico’s southwestern coast. Once the helicopter had settled onto the landing pad, he helped Jessikah out and held the box out towards her. “Phone.”

“This is ridiculous,” she grumbled loudly, but fished a phone from her purse and dropped it in the box. “What am I supposed to do for days without my phone? How am I going to take photos?”

“You’ll just have to unplug and consider it a vacation,” he said mildly.

“Vacation is when you take lots of photos!” She pouted.

“Not this time.” Dropping his own phone into the box, he secured it and handed it to the pilot. “I’ll be in touch.”

“Of course, sir. Our card. Just in case you don’t have the number committed to memory.” The pilot gave the ghost of a smile.

“Not a bad thought.” Pascal slipped the card into a pocket, reached for Jess’s hand. “Well. I don’t see anything resembling a terminal… or a welcoming committee… but there’s some shade over there. Bring our bags, please, and then you’d better make yourself scarce,” he told the pilot.

Jess promptly sat on her suitcase once they were in the shade of a large shed beside the airstrip. Pulled a pack of gum from her purse and popped a piece in her mouth. “Want some?”

“No.” He folded his arms and watched the pilot walk back to the helicopter, fly away into the bright morning. “Damn, it’s hot. Hope we won’t be waiting long.” He had to assume they were already under surveillance. There was a fair chance the pilot had also been in Fortuna’s pay, or would be bribed to reveal anything they’d talked about, too.

“Not long at all, Mr Montalban.” A door slid open beside them, and Jessikah shrieked, stumbling to her feet and grabbing at Pascal. “Apologies, miss. Didn’t mean to startle you.”

"You did startle me!" She peeped around Pascal's shoulder, and he had to bite back a laugh. He was fairly sure she wasn't acting.

The man who'd opened the door did laugh. He was dressed in a three-piece suit and tie, which had to be hot in the Puerto Rican sun, but wasn't sweating. A local, Pascal assessed; more than hired muscle, though. Some sort of factor, possibly well trusted by Fortuna. Maybe even Fortuna himself, but he didn't think so. The air of arrogance a man like Fortuna might be expected to have was lacking.

"This way, if you please." The man gestured inside the shed, a small aircraft hangar, and to a car which was parked there beside a small aircraft. "I'm Josef and I'll be escorting you to Isla Fortuna. In the back seat, if you please. Their luggage." He snapped his finger at another man, who hefted their bags into the trunk.

"We're not flying?" Jessikah asked.

"Not presently." Josef got into the drivers' seat. "We'll be leaving shortly. Please wait."

They waited in silence, watching as the other man got into the plane, taxied out of the shed and rolled away down the airstrip before taking off.

And there goes CIA's satellite tracking, Pascal thought, as Josef started the car and drove out of the shed.

Josef didn't say a word. Just drove them to a marina a few minutes' drive away and led them to a good-sized motor yacht, summoning another man to carry their bags.

"The inside cabin, please," Josef requested. "You'll find some food below. Please make yourselves comfortable."

"How long will we be on the boat?" Jessikah asked. "And do we have to stay below the whole time? I get seasick." She fluttered her lashes.

Pascal saw Josef swallow, clearly affected by her beauty. "About two hours," he said. "And yes. I am sorry. You will find medication for seasickness in the bathroom cabinet, though."

"Where are we going that'll take two hours from here?" Jess asked as they made their way below. "Are we near the US Virgin Islands?"

"Yes, but they're to the east of Puerto Rico. My guess is we're heading for the Dominican Republic, for now at least." And he was guessing they'd probably get on a helicopter or fixed-wing aircraft there, too. Fortuna was a careful man. There would be several steps to discourage anyone potentially attempting to track them. At least they could have this conversation openly; curiosity about their location was perfectly natural.

The boat got underway, moving at a fast clip, and Jess went to look for the bathroom. "I really do get seasick," she told Pascal, waving a strip of tablets at him and grabbing a bottle of mineral water from an ice bucket on the table. He suppressed a smile and nodded, taking a seat on one of the comfortable couches and looking around casually. It wasn't a huge cruiser, but the boat would probably be a cool half-million dollars' worth, and if his guess was correct, Fortuna probably never even set foot on it. It was just a decoy.

Josef came below, nodding to him politely. “Your pardon, but we must conduct the technology scans now, as you agreed.”

“And if we fail we get dropped overboard?” Pascal asked dryly.

“Of course not. The deposit you have paid will merely be kept to compensate us for the inconvenience and you will be left at our next stop, and not permitted to continue to Isla Fortuna.”

“What do you mean, our next stop? Aren’t we going to Isla Fortuna?” Jess asked.

“Hush, woman,” Pascal said firmly. “I told you. Questions aren’t for you to ask.”

She looked outraged, opened her mouth. He held up a warning finger and she snapped it shut again, flumping into a chair and sealing her lips in a thin, petulant line.

“She’s new,” Pascal said to Josef. “Still learning the ways of our world.” He affected a fond little smile. “Worth the educating, though.”

“I’ll say,” Josef murmured under his breath, stealing a sideways look at her. He nodded to Pascal. “So long as she doesn’t ask Mr Fortuna any questions he doesn't like, I'm sure there won't be a problem."

Keep your woman under control or you'll be the one who pays the price, was the unspoken subtext.

Josef opened a cabinet and pulled out several devices; Pascal recognized them all as commercially available, off-the-shelf scanning gear. He nodded in agreement when Josef asked if he could open their bags.

"My stuff..." Jess trailed off when Pascal held up a warning finger again, but then she stiffened her spine and poked her chin up. "Pascal! I don't want him poking through my underwear!"

Josef snorted with laughter. "I meant no offense," he said quickly when Pascal shot him a glare. "Here. I'll turn my back; you put your, ah, private things in this bag. Then I'll scan the outside of the bag."

Jess considered that, gave him a regal nod, accepting the compromise. One eyelid drooped in the ghost of a wink at Pascal as Josef turned his back.

What is she up to?

None of Josef's devices registered so much as a beep as he scanned their things, however, and then Jess repacked her bag while Josef scanned Pascal.

"Now hold your arms up, Jess," Pascal ordered, and she sighed and did so.

"I hope you're less gropey than the average TSA agent," she grumbled at Josef.

"I wouldn't dare touch you, miss."

Josef was as good as his word, thorough with the scans but careful never to actually touch her. He cast a couple of quick, wary sideways glances at Pascal, and Pascal decided he'd been right about Josef's place in the pecking order. More than muscle but not senior enough in Fortuna's organization to think himself above repercussions if he pissed off Fortuna's powerful, wealthy, well-connected guests.

"Thank you for your co-operation," Josef said when he'd finished, packed up his equipment and retreated. "There is food prepared in the cooler." He indicated a large built-in cooler at the back of the room. “Please, help yourselves.”

“Hungry?” Pascal asked Jess.

She shook her head. “Feeling a little queasy. The pills should kick in soon. You go ahead if you want, darling.”

He suppressed a twitch at her words, went to look in the cooler. Found a couple of elegantly prepared plates of sushi, fruit, charcuterie meats and cheeses.

“Looks like we’ll be well fed, at least.”

“Pretty,” Jess admired as he laid the plates on the table. “Pity I can’t take any pictures of it!”

“Get over yourself.” He sat back down and chose some sushi.

The journey passed quietly. A little later, Jess seemed to feel well enough to nibble on a piece of watermelon, but mostly they passed the time just gazing out of the windows, watching the shoreline of Puerto Rico recede in the distance until there was nothing but water to be seen, and then eventually land hove into view again ahead of them.

"There's an airport in Punta Cana," Pascal murmured.

"You think we'll get on another flight?"

"I reckon. If Fortuna really does have his own island. I'm reasonably familiar with the local geography and there's nothing habitable off the DR really. The Turks and Caicos islands are just to the north. Within helicopter range, anyway."

"So why didn't we fly straight there? Oh never mind, no questions. I get it."

She was even beautiful when she pouted, Pascal thought, though she gave him a fleeting instant of a grin, and he knew she was quite enjoying playing the role.

The boat docked a little while later, and another car was waiting for them. Josef drove them to the Punta Cana airport just as Pascal had guessed, but it wasn't a helicopter waiting for them, but a small private jet. They took off almost immediately and turned south instead of north as he'd expected.

An hour into the flight, Jess murmured "South America?"

"Almost has to be." They were going just about due south as far as he could tell, would be over Venezuela soon. The plane started descending for a landing, but it wasn't Caracas airport where they landed.

"Flamingo Airport?" Jess read the name off a sign on one of the buildings and laughed. "Where is that?"

"Bonaire."

"I repeat, where?"

"Near Curaçao. It's Dutch-owned."

"Are we there yet?" she sighed theatrically at Josef when he came back to collect them.

"Almost, miss." He smiled, obviously amused by her. "One more leg of the journey." He pointed to the helicopter waiting on the tarmac for them.

They were in the air again a few minutes later, heading east this time, and even Pascal's extensive knowledge of the region was becoming a bit strained. He vaguely recalled that there was a small archipelago of islands off the coast of Venezuela; it had to be where they were headed, and indeed, a little less than an hour later the helicopter set down on a smallish, rocky island with a cluster of low white buildings arranged in a semicircle around a beautiful white sand beach.

“Well I suppose the view makes up for the trip,” Jess grumbled as he helped her out of the helicopter, “but what a trip, we’ve been at it all day!”

The sun wasn’t going down yet. He shook his head at her gently for the exaggeration, took her hand on his arm and led her forward as Josef escorted them towards the largest of the buildings, another man coming up to carry their bags. The helicopter took off again immediately and Pascal wondered if it was going to collect one of the other potential buyers - and what convoluted routes they might have taken to get here.

Chapter 6

Jess was pretty sure that Isla Fortuna, whether that was its real name or not, was a former luxury hotel. Probably one that hadn't been able to sustain enough business because it was too hard to get to. She looked about as they entered the lobby, the same one they'd seen on the video; it was all open columns, marble tiles and beautifully manicured palms.

Which meant Fortuna had either taken it over very recently, or he'd kept the housekeeping and landscaping staff on at least.

"Cute," she drawled as Josef came to a stop. "I've stayed in worse. Probably. Somewhere."

"Jess," Pascal said firmly, "be quiet. We do not insult our host."

She crossed her arms, sighed and rolled her eyes, but didn't say anything else.

"I'll show you to your villa. Please be back here in the lobby by seven to meet Mr Fortuna... and I must request that you remain in your villa until then and do not wander about," Josef said, before gesturing to them to follow him again.

They followed a palm-lined path down a shallow rise, past three smaller buildings which were obviously individual villas. Josef turned off the path at a fourth, before opening the door and gesturing them to enter ahead of him.

The villa was absolutely stunning, polished wood and marble, a large bed visible through an archway off the main room, French doors opening out onto a private deck with a hot tub on it and the beach beyond that. Jessikah figured that even her Instagram model alter ego wouldn't find much to complain about, so she looked around in silence.

"Very nice," Pascal said with a nod.

"You'll find a fully equipped wet bar over there, and I hope you'll be comfortable during your stay," Josef said. "Just remember..."

"Stay here until seven. We got it."

"It's not like that's all that long," Jessikah muttered petulantly. "Since we've been traveling *all day*."

"Go take a shower," Pascal said firmly. "Might wash off some of that attitude."

She tossed her hair at him, glared at Josef and the other man just putting down their bags. "What, with those two here?"

When neither man moved, just staring at her, she put her hands on her hips and glared. "Get. Out!"

Josef jumped, spun around and hurried out, grabbing the other man and dragging him along with him. Jessikah grinned at Pascal, who immediately put his finger to his lips, then pointed to his ear and described a circle in the air.

Bugs. She nodded to show she understood. Pointed to her own ear... then to her eye.

Cameras?

Pascal shrugged. Pointed to his own eyes, then pointed around the room.

I'll look.

There was no way Jessikah was taking a shower until she knew whether she was on camera or not. Grabbing at his sleeve, she pulled him into the bathroom and gestured around.

Here first!

Pascal laughed silently, but nodded. Moved around the bathroom investigating every nook and cranny. At last, he turned back to Jess. Pointed to his eyes and shook his head. Then to his ear and shrugged.

Cameras no, audio maybe, she interpreted, and nodded. "I'm gonna take that shower," she said.

"You do that, angel."

The endearment seemed completely natural dropping from his lips, but Jess froze for a moment. Pascal didn't seem to notice, turning and leaving the bathroom, presumably to check the rest of the villa for hidden cameras.

Stripping off, she turned the shower on, grinning as jets shot out from all directions in the slate-tiled stall.

She could get used to this kind of luxury.

Although preferably without having to stay in a supervillain's lair to get it. Maybe she'd just renovate her bathroom once she got home.

Assuming she got home, that was.

With a sigh, she turned her face up to the spray of water and tried to mentally prepare herself for the much more difficult days to come.

Pascal hesitated outside the bathroom door. He was confident there were no hidden cameras in the villa after a thorough search, but audio bugs could be small and much better concealed. He had to operate on the assumption there were some.

Which meant he needed to act like he and Jess were a couple, entirely comfortable in each other's company... and he should just march casually into that bathroom like it was no big deal she was naked.

He couldn't do it. Jess might scream. So instead, he went and hefted his bag onto the bed, started unpacking it and hanging up his clothes like he was the kind of anal, Type-A guy who couldn't be seen with a crease in his shirt.

By the time he was done, Jess was coming out of the bathroom, wrapped in a towel. She gave him a quizzical look, flicked her eyes at the ceiling.

He shook his head, flicked his earlobe with his fingertip, then shrugged. She nodded and came up to him, reached up and planted a smacking kiss on his cheek.

"I'm done, darling. You take your time."

"Leave me any hot water?" He smacked the bed loudly, next to her thigh. To anyone listening it might have sounded like he smacked her bottom, and Jess caught on quickly, letting out a squeal and a giggle.

"Hey! We won't have time for that if we're going to be back in the lobby by seven. Or can we be late?" she purred.

"Better not." He lowered his own voice to a husky rasp. "Tempting though you are."

They stared at each other from a range of no more than a few inches, and Pascal suddenly found his breath coming short. Jess's eyes were so clear, so blue; she didn't look away, seemingly as transfixed as he. She licked her lips, and he didn't think she was even aware she'd done it.

For a moment he thought about kissing her. He'd have to, soon enough, to put on a show to convince Fortuna. But this would be different, just the two of them.

The silence had stretched long enough that he thought any listeners would assume they were kissing anyway. Not breaking the eye contact, he took a step back.

Jess swallowed, and he saw the sudden awareness in her eyes. That they'd come close to doing something which might have led somewhere messy.

"Get yourself unpacked," he said, "and wear something nice. I want to show you off."

"When do I ever *not* look nice?" She pretended offense.

"Well, there was that time you got too drunk to take your makeup off and woke up with raccoon eyes and bedhead," he said, deadpan.

He could see how much she wanted to laugh, but she smacked at his arm with an outraged shriek instead.

Holy shit.

The moment the bathroom door closed behind Pascal, Jessikah dropped to sit on the bed, her knees suddenly too shaky to hold her up.

Did he just almost kiss me?

It was ridiculous to feel like a giddy schoolgirl about it. They were going to *have* to kiss, multiple times and with convincing passion, over the next few days. This felt different, though. Felt like Pascal had almost kissed her just because he wanted to.

And God knows, I wouldn't have stopped him.

The more time she spent with Pascal, the more she was attracted to him. His deadpan humor, the way his whisky-gold eyes glinted with secret amusement as he glanced sideways at her, inviting her to see the comedy in their situation despite how dire it was - it was just appallingly appealing, and that wasn't even taking into account the fact that he was an extremely handsome man. Yes, he must be at least a decade Jessikah's senior, but frankly she'd never been attracted to men her own age, ever since going through high school and college several years ahead of her own peers. Men her age seemed incredibly immature to her. A man like Pascal, now... there was a man who seemed very secure of his place in the world. A man who knew what he liked and set out to get it.

Remember he's playing a role, she chided herself silently.

But role play can be fun, the devil on her shoulder whispered. *He's so very sexy when he's telling you off.*

"Ridiculous," she muttered under her breath, forcing herself to get up and unzip her case, starting to pull out dresses and take them to the closet to hang up. "Get a grip, Jess. Falling in love with this guy is a quick way to get your heart broken."

It didn't matter if anyone heard her say that. It wasn't out of character for who she was supposed to be - a girl who wasn't all that far from who Jess was herself, on paper at least. "He's rich, indulgent and hot," she said, a little louder. "You can put up with a bit of bossiness and occasional visits to whatever the hell sort of supervillain lair this is meant to be."

They had to pretend like they didn't know they were being listened to, Jessikah reasoned as she put her clothes away, humming under her breath. And the spoiled socialite she was pretending to be would have Things To Say, at least in private, about their situation.

"Hm." She selected one of the dresses, held it up in front of her, looking in the full-length mirror on the closet door. "This'll do nicely."

Pascal whistled at her when she came out the bathroom, and Jessikah didn't hide her smirk. She knew she looked amazing in the strappy white and gold Donna Karan dress, the asymmetric hem showing her entire right leg all the way to her hip, the neckline draping low in the front and even lower in back.

"I look all right, then?" she snipped at him.

"You look fucking amazing, and you know it."

She smiled, scooped up her makeup bag and swanned past him into the bathroom. "Damn right I do, sugar."

Jessikah looked even more amazing when she came out, a surprisingly short time later. She was a beautiful girl naturally, but obviously knew how to use makeup to make the most of her considerable looks when she wanted to. Her eyes looked even bigger and bluer, the delicate lines of her face subtly refined. Gold gleamed at her ears, wrists and throat.

She looked… Pascal struggled to put a word to it. *Expensive*, he finally thought. High maintenance. The kind of woman you had to treat with respect, or she'd walk away on her skyscraper designer heels and never cast you a backward glance. And she'd probably trash your reputation all over her Instagram feed while she was at it.

He smiled at the thought, before crooking his arm and angling it towards her. "Ready to go?"

"If we must. I'm starving; I hope the quality of the catering matches the accommodations." She curled her fingers around his biceps and squeezed gently. "Let's go do this, Pascal."

"Just remember," he said, "seen and not heard."

"Yes, yes, you told me," she sighed dramatically. "Only for you would I even make the effort, sugar. You'd better come through with that diamond bracelet you promised me when we get back Stateside."

"I won't forget, angel." He pressed a noisy kiss to her hair before leading her out of the villa.

"Keep your eyes out for any tech. Even wiring," Jess whispered softly as they walked back towards the main building. "I'm guessing they set up a surveillance center in the office behind what used to be the reception desk, but there has to be a little more to it than that. There are satellite dishes on the roof. Probably a server room."

"You mean you *hope* the server room isn't in the surveillance center," he whispered back cynically. "Because there will be people on the monitors the whole time."

She pinched the inside of his arm. "Just find the tech. Because until we do, nobody knows where we are. Including us!"

Jessikah had a point, Pascal thought a bit glumly. Considering their convoluted path to get here. Even he wasn't truly sure. The island chain he thought they were on was about fifty miles off Venezuela's northern coast, too far out to even see lights. The view of the night sky was incredible with no light pollution visible, pure blackness with more stars than he'd ever seen in his life glimmering high above.

"At least it's a nice place to take a vacation for a few days," he said at a more normal volume. "Enjoy the sun and the pool. Make some new friends."

She made a little huffing sound, and then laughed. "I did schedule a week's worth of Instagram posts in advance. But I also hinted I'd have a new pretty to share soon... so don't you forget that bracelet."

"You'll earn it."

He meant it, too. If they pulled this off, if they were able to intercept all three nukes and put Fortuna away... he'd damn well buy her a diamond bracelet out of his own pocket.

Chapter 7

Pascal had heard at least two more helicopters arrive while he and Jess were in their villa, and he had no idea how many others might have arrived before them. Or indeed, arrived by boat. So he wasn't surprised, when they walked into the lobby, to see several other men standing around looking at the fountains. Two, he recognized; he'd met them before. Handled deals for them. Another he knew by sight but had never met. The fourth man was a stranger.

"Mr Yoon." He nodded respectfully at the North Korean. One of the Revered Leader's right hand men, Yoon spoke no English, so far as Pascal knew, but was always accompanied by a translator. This time, a slight young

Korean woman in a military-styled tunic, her hair cut short.

"Mr Montalban," the young woman said after Yoon spoke to her quickly. "We did not expect to see you here. We have not engaged your services in this matter."

"Well, you know I do not work only for you, Mr Yoon." Pascal offered another respectful nod. "Though I hope to work with you again in the future, in this matter I'm representing a different client."

"And who might that be?" another voice snarled, this one with a heavy Eastern European accent.

Pascal turned with another smile for the barrel-chested Chechen general, who even in the sultry Caribbean heat wore full military regalia, ribbons and medals pinned across his tunic.

"Come now, General Dzhokharov. If I revealed such confidential information, I would have no more clients, would I?"

Dzhokharov humphed, but gave a slight nod of acknowledgment. “Have you met Dieter Breukel?”

“Only by reputation.” Pascal extended his hand to the man whose face he’d seen on many surveillance photos. Breukel was a Dutchman and, like Pascal Montalban, a broker. A middleman.

“Similarly.” Breukel shook his hand with a polite nod, his eyes sharp as he sized Pascal up. Just as the other men had, he flicked a brief, appreciative glance up and down Jessikah and then just as obviously, dismissed her from his thoughts.

“And the last of our merry band.” Dzhokharov pointed to the last man, who remained a little apart from them. “Saul Hayworth.”

Pascal felt Jess’s fingers tighten fractionally on his arm. The name meant absolutely nothing to him, but he guessed she’d heard it before. The man looked and dressed like an American.

“I’ve seen him on TV,” she spoke up. “His daddy’s Joshua Hayworth, right? The televangelist?”

“You’d better not call him that.” Dzhokharov laughed richly. “Hayworth thinks he’s the second coming of Christ himself, and all his disciples agree with him... including his son.”

A fundamentalist cult leader type. And presumably, a very well funded one. “The fire and brimstone type of preacher?” Pascal queried.

“He sure is. If he’s a buyer, I wanna know where he’s planning to use it. Just so I can plan to be very far away,” Jess said, turning wide eyes to him, and he nodded.

“I understand your concern, angel. We’ll see. Maybe he’ll do us the professional courtesy of suggesting a safe place to be.”

“New Zealand, perhaps.” Dzhokharov laughed again, and Pascal thought that the Chechen had already been in the alcohol. Or perhaps something stronger. He seemed a little too excited, almost manic.

“My friends,” a voice boomed through the lobby, and they all turned to see another man entering, accompanied by Josef and two other men. Dressed all in white, the new arrival spread his arms in welcome.

"Welcome to Isla Fortuna Continental. I am your host… Baz Fortuna."

It was all Pascal could do not to let his mouth drop open with shock. Because he knew who the man in white really was, and his name wasn't Baz Fortuna.

"Pascal?" Jess murmured, as Baz Fortuna made his way around the room, shaking hands and greeting his guests. "What is it? You've gone all stiff."

"He's a former CIA agent. Supposedly dead. Sebastian Maroney." Pascal spoke quietly, never taking his eyes off Maroney, or Fortuna, or whatever he was calling himself now.

"Former CIA!"

"He won't know who I am." Pascal flicked his eyes sideways at her. "There is no occasion on which we would have met. He supposedly died seven years ago."

Before Pascal joined the Agency, Jess immediately understood, and nodded. She'd never heard Maroney's name, which meant the Agency almost certainly didn't have the faintest clue Maroney was still alive and had turned to the dark side. Dead heroes didn't get talked about nearly as much as live supervillains.

It also made sense why 'Baz Fortuna' avoided in-person meetings where at all possible. He needed to stay off the CIA's radar even more completely than most. One photo of him meeting with a known bad guy and his picture would be fed into the sophisticated facial recognition algorithms Jess had helped to program when she was at NSA. Even being reported dead wouldn't keep them from identifying him then. He was hardly the first bad actor to fake his own death, after all. NSA had learned that lesson the hard way.

"Pascal Montalban." Fortuna came to stand in front of them, his smile broad and blindingly white. "Your reputation precedes you. As does mine, obviously." He laughed loudly, before giving Jess a long, considering inspection. "And who do we have here?"

Picking up her hand, he brought it to his lips and kissed it lingeringly.

"Jessica Berry-Sandford." She smiled at him, flashing dimples. "Is this your island, Baz... may I call you Baz? It's charming."

"You may call me anything you like." His eyes were all over her, noting her clothes, her jewelry, the quality of her manicure. "I like your shoes, Jessica."

"Do you? Louboutins." She kicked up one red sole. "Did you know they made espadrille wedges? I found them at Nordstrom. Too cute."

"I like their sneakers, myself." He gestured down at his own feet, shod in white sneakers with jaggedly spiked red soles. "Loubisharks."

She made herself let out a delighted trill of laughter. "A man of good taste!"

"I hope you'll continue to think me so. Josef." Fortuna beckoned to his aide. "Open the doors, please."

Josef hurried to obey, opening a pair of double doors on one side of the lobby, admitting the group to a large function room, set up as a dining room with a single long table down the center and a fully equipped bar at one side. Several women in skimpy dresses were clustered at the bar.

"Gentlemen. And ladies. Please, come in to dinner."

"We aren't here to dine," the Korean translator spoke up, obviously prompted by Mr Yoon. "When will the auction take place?"

"All in good time, my friend." Fortuna smiled his shark's grin, his eyes black and dead. "For tonight, I hope you'll enjoy the hospitality of Isla Fortuna Continental. You all understand the significance of the name, I trust? You've seen *John Wick*?"

The Continental. Neutral ground. Jess didn't nod, but she saw Pascal incline his head, Breukel as well, and Hayworth. Yoon and Dzhokharov looked blank, and Josef and one of Fortuna's other aides sidled up to them, obviously to explain the concept.

"Some of you have brought your own companionship," Fortuna said, "but please... do allow my friends to entertain you as well." He gestured to the women at the bar, who moved forward at the obviously pre-arranged signal, offering glasses of champagne and practiced smiles.

The Korean translator with Yoon backed off a pace, distaste curling her thin lips, but Yoon didn't seem to care or notice. For the first time, Jess realized there was a woman with Dzhokharov as well... a girl really, thin and slight in a shimmering silver dress which barely skimmed the tops of her thighs. She was following close behind the Chechen general, staying within arms' reach as though tethered to him, her eyes cast down to the floor. Dzhokharov didn't seem to take any notice of her, grinning broadly and making boisterous remarks as Fortuna's women approached him.

"Thank you," Jess accepted a glass of champagne, took a sip and hummed appreciatively. The expensive stuff, she thought. Considering the size of the non-refundable deposits the bidders had paid to be here, though, Fortuna could afford to lay it on. Her payment had been the largest at just under a quarter of a million dollars, but it would be over a million dollars between the four of them, which would cover all the expenses of getting everyone here and entertaining them at least.

A door on the other side of the room opened, and staff began to file into the room carrying platters of food, laying them on the table. Fortuna urged his guests to take seats, and a little to Jess's surprise, as she sat down beside Pascal she found Fortuna taking the seat on her other side. His attention was immediately monopolized by Dzhokharov who sat down opposite, though, so she tried to let go of her tension and enjoy the admittedly excellent food.

The girl in the silver dress had taken a seat by Dzhokharov and sat with her hands in her lap and her eyes cast down, nibbling at a couple of bites of the food Dzhokharov put on her plate and not speaking. Jess considered her options, briefly, decided that her persona would at least make an effort to be friendly, and during a lull in the conversation, leaned forward and spoke.

"Hi, I'm Jess. What's your name?"

The girl's eyes flew up to Jess's face. She looked startled at being spoken to.

"Oh… sorry… do you not speak English? I don't speak Russian. *Parlez-vous français*?"

"I speak a little English," the girl said hesitantly, after casting a brief sideways glance at Dzhokharov, who ignored her, speaking to the woman on his other side. "My name, Mariska."

"It's nice to meet you, Mariska." Jess was about to ask another question when Fortuna butted in.

"You speak French, Jess?"

"Of course." She batted her eyelashes at him. "It's where Pascal and I met. Daddy has a chalet at Val d'Isère; we go there every spring to ski."

"I see. What does your father do, would I have heard of him?"

"I doubt it! He's a currency trader." She giggled, waved her fingertips airily. "Spends his days buried in graphs on computer screens. He's *very* good at it."

The implication, of course, being that he was *very* rich. And if Fortuna sent his people looking, they'd find a perfect electronic record for one Emmanuel Sandford, net wealth in the high eight figures.

There was no such person in real life, but it would take at least a few days and the expenditure of significant resources to figure that out, and by that time - if Fortuna even bothered - Jessikah hoped they'd be long gone.

"You're not interested in following in your father's footsteps?" Fortuna pressed.

Jess gave him a blank look. "Why would I? He's a bore. Half the time even when we're in Val d'Isère he's too busy working to come out and enjoy the slopes. I'd rather enjoy my life."

"This is a woman who knows how to live," Pascal joined the conversation, putting his arm around her shoulders. "Fearless! You should have seen her on that black diamond run. I couldn't catch her, and I was trying. Do you ski, Fortuna?"

"On occasion. Never been to Val d'Isère, though. Perhaps I'll try it out." Fortuna never took his eyes off Jess; she could feel her skin crawling under the intensity of his stare, but kept her expression blithe, unconcerned.

"We're always there at Easter. Perhaps we'll see you next year. Pascal, sugar, my glass is empty." She turned away, needing to break eye contact at least briefly before she slipped up and showed her revulsion.

"My staff are failing me." Fortuna's expression darkened; he snapped his fingers and pointed to Jess's glass. A sever almost fell over himself in his rush to refill it, his expression panicked.

"Don't let that happen again," Fortuna snarled.

"Yes, sir!"

"My guests expect attentive service. See that you deliver it." Fortuna sighed, obviously dismissing the man from his attention. "My apologies, my dear."

"No offense taken, sugar. My compliments on the champagne, by the way. Delightful. As is the food!"

"It's killing her not to be able to take photos for her Instagram," Pascal told Fortuna.

"Ah… I'm sorry about that, Jessica. Of course, you must understand the sensitive nature of my business. And the privacy of my guests must be respected, too."

She gave a theatrical sigh, rolling her eyes, but added a smile to show she was play-acting. "It's fine. It's your place, Mr Fortuna. Your rules."

"You're a smart woman." His eyes were surprisingly warm as he looked at her. "It's rare to find a woman who looks like you do and has a brain to match. You've got a good one here, Montalban. I hope you appreciate her."

"Oh, I do," Pascal said, even as Jessikah silently simmered over Fortuna's misogynistic comment.

Fortuna kept *touching* her. A light squeeze on the shoulder, a pat on the hand, the brush of his thigh against hers as he manspreaded in his chair. It could only be deliberate, because he wasn't doing it to the woman on his other side, and it was everything Jess could do not to flinch away with every touch. Every instinct was telling her to grab one of his fingers and bend it back until he squealed next time, but that was the last thing she could do. When he put his hand on her thigh, though, she had to do something.

"Excuse me, y'all." She shoved her chair back and rose to her feet. "I need to visit the little girls' room."

"Allow me to show you..." Fortuna pushed back his chair and made to rise, but she put a hand on his shoulder, laughing.

"Sugar, I can see the sign right over there! Ain't gonna get lost. Back in a minute, toots." She blew Pascal a kiss and sashayed away, too aware of Fortuna's eyes on her back.

Chapter 8

Pascal was well aware that Fortuna getting handsy with Jess was a power play. A way to demonstrate his dominance, to stamp his authority and show that everything on the island was his for the taking. And the reality of the situation was that if Fortuna decided he wanted Jess and he was going to take her, there was nothing Pascal could do. He was outnumbered, and considering he was completely unarmed, outgunned too. About all he could do was get himself killed or beaten insensible, which would leave Jess with no backup.

He had to trust Jess to handle Fortuna herself. Or hope one of the other women would distract Fortuna suitably; the stunning brunette seated on Fortuna's other side was certainly trying, leaning into him as she pressed her elbows together, making her breasts literally fall out of the top of her skimpy red dress.

Jess came back from the bathroom then, and looking at the way she walked, the white and gold dress clinging to her sinuous curves, Pascal admitted to himself that even in a room with ten other beautiful women, Jess drew every eye.

He had to do something, or she was going to be harassed by all of them, not just Fortuna. Had to put his stamp of possession on her, such that at least the other potential buyers would think twice, for fear of pissing him off.

Rising to his feet as Jess returned to the table, Pascal held his hand out towards her, trying to telegraph his intentions. She took his hand, a question in her eyes, and he pulled her close, hooking his other hand around her waist and pressing their bodies together from chest to hip.

"*Oh,*" she said silently, her eyes flicked sideways very briefly, and he saw her brain click into gear, computing what he was doing, and why.

And then her lips curved into a mysterious little smile and she leaned in closer, reaching up towards him, her eyelashes drifting down to rest on her cheeks.

It was tacit permission, and he took it, slanting his mouth over hers and kissing her long, slow and thoroughly.

They were too close to the others to make it anything but a real kiss, and Jessikah was either a superb actress or thoroughly enjoying herself, because she kissed him back thoroughly, melting against him and running the fingers of her free hand into his hair.

It was the kind of kiss that could knock a man's world off its axis entirely, and for several long seconds, Pascal forgot all about the other people in the room. The terrorists and petty tyrants he'd dedicated his life to bringing down, watching each other avidly for chinks in the armor, anything they might use to bring each other down, like a pack of hyenas.

Jess wasn't his weakness, though. She was a strength. They would underestimate her, see her as just a beautiful face and body, and never for a moment guess at the brilliant mind behind it.

He ended the kiss slowly, lifting his head, and Jess blinked her eyes open, smiled that mysterious little smile again, and startled him by deliberately scritching her nails down the back of his neck. He jumped slightly, goosebumps rising all over his body.

"Now sugar," she said, her voice pitched just loud enough for Fortuna to hear. "You know you don't have to get jealous over me talkin' to other men. I'm all yours."

"And don't you forget it." He slapped her behind lightly, then let go of her and held the back of her chair for her to take her seat.

Fortuna was watching them, his expression still and thoughtful, and then as soon as Pascal met his gaze, his expression changed, back to the expansive, generous host, full of bonhomie.

"Desserts!" Fortuna cried, and the servers came hurrying out from the kitchen, bearing several trays and platters with elaborate desserts atop them. “You must try the bombe Alaska, my friends. A most appropriate dessert for this gathering, I thought!” He laughed loudly, inviting them to join him in his mirth, and Pascal and Jessikah dutifully joined in.

Mariska, the Chechen girl, was watching them. Dzhokharov was getting drunk, as usual in Pascal’s experience - the man had no discipline - and already had one of Fortuna’s girls in his lap, about which Mariska looked relieved. Pascal had the extremely uneasy feeling that she was even younger than she looked.

He’d seen a lot of horrible things in the last few years, and had to look the other way more often than not. He had the distinct feeling, though, that Jessikah wasn’t going to be able to do that. Not if her narrowed gaze as she watched the way Mariska flinched away from Dzhokharov’s extravagant gestures was any guide.

“Remember why we’re here,” he said softly into her ear, under the guise of nibbling sensually at it. “A little Chechen girl isn’t it.”

"Little girl, exactly," Jess whispered back, but he saw the resignation as she glanced up at him. She understood.

Three nukes trumped any individual's welfare. Once they were secured, if he could do something for Mariska, he would, but until then, they had to stay on mission.

"Well, I'm full," he declared, "and after today, I think I'm for bed. Might take a walk first, if you don't mind, Fortuna? Out of courtesy, is there anywhere that's off-limits? Don't want to tread on any toes."

"Good of you to ask, Montalban." Fortuna inclined his head in thanks for the professional courtesy. "The villa at the top of the hill is mine; don't go past the gate in the fence surrounding it. Should one of my guards tell you to stop, please do so, but otherwise you may go anywhere on the island you please."

"And tomorrow, we do business?"

"In the afternoon." Fortuna smiled wolfishly. "I think some of my guests wouldn't take too kindly if I required an early start." He flicked a quick glance across the table at Dzhokharov, and, perhaps surprisingly, Hayworth, the preacher's son, who also appeared quite drunk, with a girl in his lap. Or perhaps not so surprisingly. Maybe Hayworth was kept on a tight leash by his father normally.

Or perhaps the Hayworths were both massive hypocrites who didn't practice what they preached, which was just as likely, Pascal thought as he rose to his feet, drawing Jess up with him.

"And good night to you, my dear," Fortuna said to Jess, reaching out to catch her hand and placing a lingering kiss on the back of it. "Unless you'd like to ditch the dull Mr Montalban and stay at the party? I'd make it worth your while."

"Oh, sugar." She laughed teasingly, withdrawing her hand. "You can't afford me."

Oh shit. It had been the wrong thing to say. Pascal saw the challenge light go on in Fortuna's eyes. There was nothing he could say to mitigate the damage right now, though, so he smiled blandly and drew Jessikah out of the room with him.

"Shit," she whispered as they walked out into the gardens. "I think I just fucked up."

"I can fix it, but I'm going to have to go back and talk to him alone. I need to anyway. He wants you and he's not being subtle about it."

"What the hell are you going to say?" she hissed.

"I'm still figuring that out," he admitted. "But if I don't do it, he's going to decide you're too much of a challenge to resist and he's just going to order his men to kill me to get me out of the way. I need to get him thinking with his business brain rather than the head in his pants."

"He's got to be smart, if he was Agency and he's managed to stay off their radar for years." Jess looked thoughtful, as they strolled through the gardens lit by tiki torches flaring here and there in the darkness, heads bent towards each other like lovers exchanging sweet nothings. "If I didn't know that, I'd think he was all ego and flash."

"I've been wracking my brain trying to remember what I know about him. He disappeared in South America somewhere, might even have been Venezuela. The Agency got a video of him being tortured and killed, if I remember right."

"Must have been a hell of a deepfake. I'd like to take a look."

"No doubt." Pascal shook his head ruefully. "They assumed it was true because it was what they expected to see, but he must have set it all up himself, the bastard."

"We'll get him. I'll make sure your boss knows who he is, once we find the computers and can get word out."

"Yeah." Pascal didn't like their chances, but he didn't say anything. The men accompanying Fortuna were carrying radios, not cellphones, and he'd seen no telltale rectangles in any pockets. Fortuna was smart to control whatever tech had to be on the island tightly, but it was going to make their lives difficult and dangerous, and very possibly they'd only ever get one chance to get a message out. They had to pick their moment carefully.

They'd arrived back at their villa, and Pascal opened the door for Jess to enter. "I'd better go back and speak with him. Don't want to leave it until morning. He'll be simmering over that 'can't afford me' remark."

"I'm sorry," she said, contrite.

"It's all right, angel. Just stay here. I'll be back soon." He gave her a smacking kiss on the cheek for their potential audience to hear, before turning on his heel.

Josef came to his side as Pascal returned to the dining room. "Everything all right, Mr Montalban? Is there something you and Miss Berry-Sandford require in your villa?"

"I need a private word with Mr Fortuna. Not about the business matter which has us all here. A personal thing."

Josef gave him raised eyebrows.

"I think my girlfriend inadvertently said something to Mr Fortuna which may have caused offense. I want to ensure it is made right," Pascal elaborated.

"Come this way."

Josef led him back into the lobby, and across the other side to a small lounge which had probably once been used by travelers waiting for their pickup. “I’ll ask if Mr Fortuna will see you,” Josef said, before leaving him alone.

Pascal guessed Fortuna would keep him waiting, so he took the opportunity to amble, apparently casually, around the room and surreptitiously look everything over very thoroughly.

And that was when he saw it. Through the window, he was looking out across a sort of service passageway at the back of the main hotel building, and he could see through a lighted window into another room. One where there were computers. Several of them.

He moved around to the other side of the window subtly, trying to see if there was anyone in the computer room, but it appeared to be empty. He could see a door from this side; tried to work out where it would exit to.

“Mr Montalban,” a voice said behind him, and he turned to see Fortuna, hands in the pockets of his white pants, a small smirk on his face. “What can I do for you? I’m not prepared to talk business without the other buyers present, in the interests of fairness."

"Understood. That's not what this is about." Pascal stood tall and looked the other man in the eye. "This is between you and me."

"It is?" Fortuna tilted his head, smiled curiously. "So far as I know, tonight's the first time we've ever met, though I've heard of you, of course. We have occasional mutual clients in common."

"Indeed, but I think Jessica may have managed to inadvertently offend you." Pascal shrugged. "With that comment about not being able to afford her."

"For a moment, perhaps. But then I thought about it and realized... she's not the kind of woman you can buy, is she?"

"Her daddy's probably worth more than you and I combined. And he didn't make it all legally, despite how neat and tidy everything might look now. He got his seed money laundering for the cartels." Pascal was embellishing, but he needed to give Fortuna a reason to back off without losing face. "*I* wouldn't risk pissing him off. Jess is his only child, and while she might talk shit on him and call him a boring nerd, they adore each other. Anything happens to her, he'd spend every cent to hunt down whoever was responsible and call it well spent."

"Ah," Fortuna murmured.

"I'm going to speak plainly. I can see you're attracted to her. Every red-blooded man who's laid eyes on her since I met her has been attracted to her." He smiled ruefully, inviting Fortuna to share his amusement. "But the thing is, she's not a woman you can buy, or take, or claim. She's a woman you have to win. And I did." He hardened his tone, staring Fortuna in the eye. "And with all due respect, I don't appreciate you putting your hands on what's mine. Your hospitality doesn't entitle you to that."

"Oh come now." Fortuna tried to laugh it off.

"This is your home and your rules, I respect that. Business comes first for both of us, I think, and I hope to do business with you on this deal, and perhaps more in the future. But the respect has to be mutual and there's clearly none coming my way if you're trying to make a move on Jess right in front of me."

For a fraught moment, they stared at each other in silence. Pascal could almost see the wheels turning in Fortuna's mind, as the deeply selfish, arrogant arms dealer ran mental calculations. Trying to figure out if he could have everything he wanted without expensive and possibly devastating repercussions.

In the end, Fortuna shrugged and laughed. "What's the issue, Montalban? She's just a woman."

"*My* woman."

"Whatever you say. I'm going back to *my* party. Enjoy your evening." Fortuna turned on his heel and walked away without another word, leaving Pascal wondering whether he'd just made things better or worse.

Chapter 9

It took Jess approximately three minutes alone in the villa to decide she didn't want to be there. And less than one minute more to whip off her dress and shoes and drag on a pair of yoga pants, a tank top and a stocking cap... all black, all of which she'd had concealed in the 'underwear bag' she hadn't allowed Josef to examine earlier. Black pumps completed her sneaking-around outfit and she was ready to go.

There were computers somewhere on this damn island. And she was going to find them.

She slipped silently out into the night, stepping immediately off the torchlit paths and relying on the bright moonlight and starlight to find her way around.

"Back in the main building, it has to be," she whispered to herself. "But around the back... maybe behind the kitchens?"

She worked her way around to the back of the building. Almost tripped over a garbage can and caught herself against the wall just in time, her breath hissing out. Not a moment too soon, because a door suddenly swung open and a kitchen worker came out, slinging another bag into the trash, muttering to himself the whole while.

Jess didn't even dare breathe. Just stood pressed against the wall, hoping the shadows hid her sufficiently.

The man turned and went back into the kitchen, and Jess let out a breath. That had been too close. If she hadn't almost fallen over the bin, she'd have walked right into him, and she had absolutely no explanation that would have passed muster as to why she was skulking around the service alley in the dark.

She crept on, past the kitchen door, towards two lighted windows on either side of the alley. Voices from the window on the right stopped her before she got there.

That was Pascal's voice. And Fortuna's. She'd stumbled onto what sounded like the tail end of a conversation.

"What's the issue, Montalban? She's just a woman." That was Fortuna's voice, cold and scornful.

"*My* woman," Pascal said, quiet but firm.

"Whatever you say. I'm going back to my party. Enjoy your evening."

Fortuna's Loubisharks squeaked slightly as he turned on his heel and walked out.

Jess took a chance and peeked in the window, saw only Pascal's back as he too exited the room.

My woman.

She wasn't quite sure how she felt about that. Her stomach was squirming weirdly. Of course it was all an act from Pascal, but... that kiss earlier had sure felt real.

My woman.

Part of her wanted it to be real.

Loud laughter reached her ears from the party two rooms away, and Jess shook herself. Standing here mooning over Pascal wasn't serving her purpose.

Turning around, she stepped carefully across the alleyway and crouched below the sill of the other window, lifting up to peep through with one eye.

Yes! She allowed herself a little fist pump. She'd found the computers. And they were good ones; her experienced eye spied servers, a satellite link and more. No surveillance equipment, though. As she'd suspected, that had to be in a different room and probably on an internal server, isolated from the larger internet. That's how she'd have done it, anyway. And Fortuna had been CIA trained, he was no fool. Access to the server room was probably tightly controlled... there was nobody in there right now. Carefully, she felt around the window, but it was sealed, not designed to open easily if at all. She needed to find where the door on the other side of the room led out to, but not tonight, because Pascal would be getting back to the villa any moment, and when he found her missing, he'd be straight back here kicking up a fuss.

She ran all the way back on silent feet, staying away from the lit paths, and met Pascal just as he was walking up to the villa. He took one look at her in her black outfit and stocking cap, and his lips tightened.

Oh dear, I'm in trouble. She grinned wickedly at him. "Found the server room," she mouthed at him triumphantly.

"So did I," he mouthed back.

Oh. He'd probably seen it through that other window. She drooped, crestfallen, as she realized she'd risked sneaking out for absolutely nothing.

Pascal's face softened, and he reached out, swiping the stocking cap off her hair, and stuffing it in his pocket. "I talked to Fortuna," he said, speaking out loud for the benefit of any unseen listeners. "Made it clear respect has to go both ways."

"You're being silly," she said, taking her cue from him. "He was just flirting. I could handle it."

"Maybe. He's not a man used to being denied what he wants, but he has to understand trying to take you comes with consequences, and not just from me."

Jess raised her eyebrows curiously, and Pascal… did he actually look *sheepish*? What had he said to Fortuna, before the little bit she'd overheard?

"I told him your father could buy us both out of pocket change… and that he got his start money laundering for the cartels."

Jess blinked, startled, and then she grinned. Pascal couldn't know it, but that was a touch of genius which would explain any surface irregularities which might show up if Fortuna set his people to looking into her fictional father.

"Now sugar," she purred, looping her arms around his neck, "you know I'm not supposed to tell anybody about that. Daddy's one hundred per cent respectable these days."

"Who's Fortuna going to tell, angel? I just wanted him to understand it's not just me he'd be messing with if he lets his cock rule his thinking."

"You're being possessive. And I rather like it."

Jess was beginning to lose track of what she was play-acting for their unseen audience and what she was really feeling. This undercover shit was confusing as hell; how had Liane lived like this for years? Jess had been undercover for *one day* and was already exhausted.

"Come on," Pascal said. "Take your makeup off and let's go to bed."

A good idea, but she already knew they couldn't go straight to sleep. They'd have to act out at least the sounds of lovemaking, to avoid making anyone suspicious; they'd discussed it on the long drive to San Diego, concluding that they had to stay in character from the moment they landed in Puerto Rico in case they were observed.. Jess blew out a little sigh and nodded, meeting Pascal's gaze.

"Five minutes."

He nodded, turning away and pulling his shirt off over his head. She stared, transfixed, as muscles in his back rippled under smooth brown skin, before shaking herself out of it and heading for the bathroom.

Get a grip, she ordered herself silently as she swept a cleansing wipe over her face. *Yes, he's a fit, attractive man and he kisses like a dream, but...*

There were no buts, she realized dismally. Her libido was absolutely not listening. Something inside her was wildly turned on by everything about Pascal and she couldn't switch it off with cold hard logic.

Maybe it was the constant threat of discovery, too, she mused as she brushed her teeth. The added element of danger had adrenalin coursing through her veins constantly, heightening every sensation and reaction.

"You done, Jess?" Pascal said quietly outside the bathroom door.

"Just about." She flushed the toilet, washed her hands, and opened the door.

He looked her up and down and grinned. "Nice."

She'd changed into the pajamas she brought with her, a tank top and loose pants in a silky material. They covered her completely, but the expensive, slippery fabric would have made them look like sexy lingerie in her suitcase.

"Glad you like them," she said pertly.

"You'd look stunning in a potato sack and you know it."

The door closed behind him and Jess tried to fight down the warm flush flooding her at the compliment. She went and got into bed, rearranging the pillows and tossing a bunch of decorative cushions to the floor.

"Who could sleep with this many pillows?" she muttered derisively. "Give me comfort over aesthetics any day." Wiggling about, she discovered that at least the mattress was comfortable. And the air-conditioning was set to a sane temperature, so she'd be able to sleep, if her racing mind would settle down enough to let her, at least.

Pascal came out of the bathroom wearing just a pair of boxer shorts, switching the overhead light off on his way over to the bed. Jess reached out to turn off the lamp next to her, but he shook his head.

"No, leave it on. I want to see your face."

He wanted to check that anything he did was okay with her, she understood him to mean, and he needed to be able to see visual cues since she might not be able to give him verbal ones for fear of making listeners suspicious.

"You looked a million bucks tonight," Pascal said softly, slipping into bed beside her. "That dress was worth every cent of whatever you paid for it."

"Not a million bucks. I promise. But if you will give a girl your credit card and let her loose on Rodeo Drive?" She giggled. "You've got to expect a bit of damage."

"Worth it." He leaned on his side, looking at her. "I know you're used to being spoiled by your doting daddy. I assure you, I'll keep you in the style to which you're accustomed."

"I know. Are you still worried I'm going to be tempted away by the guy with his own private island?" she said teasingly. "Darling. I've been propositioned by probably twenty guys with their own private islands. My best friend from school is freaking European royalty. I'm hard to impress."

“Remind me again why you’re here with me?”

“Because you offered me something money can’t buy.” She reached out and touched his face. *Adventure*, she mouthed, her eyes sparkling, but aloud she said “Sincerity.”

He shook his head, his own eyes dark with emotion she couldn’t name. Concern, she suspected. Worry that she, with her lack of undercover experience, would stumble recklessly into something and compromise them both.

Look at tonight. She should have waited for him to get back, not run off at the first opportunity and risked exposure, just to find out something Pascal already knew. They needed to better co-ordinate their efforts, and Jess knew she was in the wrong. Her expertise was in the tech. That was the reason she was here. Pascal was the spy, and she needed to leave the spying to him unless he assigned her a specific task.

“Ready?” he mouthed at her, and she nodded.

Pascal put his hand to his mouth, kissed the back of it, loudly.

Jess choked down a laugh. Made a soft moan instead.

Pascal thumped a hand against the headboard. The bed squeaked and he grinned.

They alternated rocking back and forth, making the bed squeak, both having to hold back laughter, trying instead to moan and groan in a convincing imitation of sex.

Jess buried her face in the pillow, unable to keep from laughing any longer. Pascal stroked her shaking shoulders lightly, pressing between her shoulder blades. She risked a glance at him, saw the grin on his face, and had to stuff a corner of the pillow into her mouth. Little squeaks and squeals emerged, and the thought that anyone listening might think those were noises she might make during sex just made her laugh harder. Tension released, she found tears running down her cheeks.

"There's my beautiful girl," Pascal murmured, stroking her shoulder. "You're doing so good."

The words could have fit either situation, but she knew he was reassuring her about her blunder earlier. Her fieldwork inexperience.

Impulsively, she rolled to her side and put her arm over him in a hug. “I’m so glad I’m here with you,” she whispered, not sure whether any hidden microphones would pick her up or not and not caring.

Pascal froze for a moment, and then his big hand moved up to gently smooth over her hair. “There is nobody else I would want here with me to get this done,” he said quietly.

She smiled, gazing into his eyes, and something changed between them. Lying side by side, touching already, it was as though the air between them suddenly became charged.

Jess licked her lips, entirely unconsciously, and Pascal drew in a sharp breath. His fingers curled in her hair, cradling her head. Drawing her just the tiniest bit closer, but the pressure was so light, she knew she could easily pull back if she wanted to.

Every ounce of common sense she possessed was screaming at her that she should pull back. That this was a Bad Idea, that the lines between personal and business relationship were already messily blurred in this situation.

She kissed him anyway. Jess had never been very good at denying herself something she really wanted, and right now, she wanted to kiss Pascal more than just about anything she'd ever wanted in her life.

He groaned for real this time as the kiss deepened, and she was moaning too, because this kiss was even more perfect, even hotter, than the one they'd performed for an audience in the dining room earlier.

Jess dug her fingers into his shoulder, dragging herself closer to him, pressing her body up against the length of his. He was hard, his cock pressing against the thin fabric of his shorts, pushing against her belly. Her body's reaction wasn't as obvious, but her nipples were hard little nubs pushing into his chest, and the wetness between her thighs made her want to squirm her loose pants off and ride him until they both screamed.

She wasn't quite sure who pulled back. Perhaps they both had a collective attack of sanity, but somehow their lips parted and they were staring into each others' eyes, breathing fast, their pulses thundering.

"Jess," he said quietly, and then he shook his head. "You make me feel… too much. I need to keep my mind on… business."

He was right. They both needed to keep their minds on the job, the reason they were here. There was far too much at stake for them to get distracted.

"When we go home," she said quietly, "I think maybe there are some serious conversations we should have. About the future."

"You deserve that. But this deal is too important. To me, to my client. I need to focus."

"I understand. I promise, I'll… behave myself. Not distract you."

He laughed suddenly, golden eyes sparkling. "You are a distraction by existing, Jess, but that's not on you. It's on me to keep my focus."

"Me too," she said quietly.

He nodded, expression turning serious, but out loud he said "Oh angel, you just focus on having a good time while we're here. Take in some sunshine. Maybe make friends with some of the other girls."

"Talking of which," she said, "how old do you think that little Russian girl is?"

"Chechen. Dzhokharov is Chechen, and I'm betting the girl is too. Don't get involved, Jess."

"She can't be eighteen!" Jess wasn't playacting her outrage.

"Don't. Get. Involved. We're not here for her."

"*You're* not here for her. I've got money. Resources. If I wanted to help her..."

"Dzhokharov will kill you without a second thought. Fortuna might reconsider his options after the consequences being explained to him, but Dzhokharov doesn't think the same way, and he's backed by the president of his country. Don't. Get. Involved."

Chapter 10

The mere thought of Dzhokharov deciding to blot Jess from existence out of mere irritation - which was all the loss of Mariska would likely mean to the Chechen general - made Pascal's blood run cold.

"I know you're outraged. But you need to develop a thicker skin if you want to live in my world. And you know I want you here."

"I know. You know I've seen shit. I've got no problem with you making money the way that you do. But I draw the line at *children*."

He knew she wouldn't be talked out of it. That she'd try to find some way to help Mariska, no matter what.

And, of course, if they managed to get away, Dzhokharov would never find her to take his revenge, because Jessica Berry-Sandford didn't exist.

"When the deal is done," he said, "I'll talk to Dzhokharov. Can't promise anything, but the way he was looking at Fortuna's women - maybe he doesn't care that much about Mariska. I'll offer him some incentive, imply I maybe have an interested buyer for her. He'd never let her go if he thought I wanted her for myself, but with you around that's not something he'd assume anyway."

"Thank you," she said, nestling against his chest, tucking her head under his chin. "I appreciate that, Pascal."

He sighed, breathing in the scent of her hair as he reached to switch the lamp off. "Just gotta get this deal done, Jess."

"I know." She nudged his chest with her nose. "*We'll* get it done," she whispered.

She seemed to fall asleep within minutes, from the way her breathing slowed and she went limp against him. Pascal, however, lay awake for hours, staring into the darkness, worrying about all the ways things could go wrong. About the potential for disaster on an unprecedented scale if he and Jess failed.

And yes, about working with a woman who was completely untried in the field and not even employed by the US Government.

At least, he thought she wasn't. He still wasn't entirely clear about what Hestia Global Security actually was, and he could hardly ask her now.

She sighed in her sleep and snuggled tighter against him, and Pascal swore under his breath as his traitorous body reacted yet again to her closeness. He'd lost count of the number of gorgeous women who'd draped themselves over him in the course of his undercover work over the last few years, and never, not even once, had he ever had a physical reaction like this, completely out of his own control.

He must have fallen asleep at some point, because he woke in the cool light of early morning as Jess slipped out of his arms.

"Too early to get up," he murmured, and she laughed quietly.

"Bathroom break. Back in a minute."

"Mmkay." He let his eyes close again, and was drifting back to sleep when she slid back into bed and warmed cold feet up on his shins, giggling at his grumbled complaint.

The next time he woke, she was sitting at the dressing-table brushing out her hair.

Lying back against the pillows, he put his hands behind his head and just watched. She'd changed out of her pajamas into a loose, short sundress with a halter neck, and he suspected she had a bikini or swimsuit on beneath it.

Glancing at him in the mirror, she smiled. "Good morning, sleepy."

"*Bonjour, cherie*." He slipped into French, something he did regularly while undercover. His character had supposedly grown up in a Marseilles slum, after all. He had to admit he was curious just how good Jess's French was, too. He doubted she'd have made the claims she had about visiting France annually if she couldn't back it up when pressed, but obviously her family didn't actually own a ski chalet in Val d'Isère.

Or did they? He knew next to nothing about the real Jessikah Hagerty, after all.

She cast him an amused glance and replied in the same language, asking how he had slept.

“Well enough. And you?”

“Always well, when I’m with you.” She finished brushing her hair, set the brush aside, and reached up to separate out strands and weave a complicated braid that wound around the back of her head and left a single plait hanging over one shoulder.

“How the hell do you do that without seeing it?” he wondered, making her laugh.

“Lots of practice, darling!” Tying the end off with an elastic, she rose and came over to the bed, leaning over to brush a kiss on his cheek. “I’m starving, and there’s only snacks in the fridge. Do you think we’ll find some breakfast at the main building?”

“Undoubtedly.”

“Shall I meet you there, then?”

“You shall absolutely not go anywhere without me,” he said in a warning tone, and she sighed and sat down on the end of the bed.

"Then I guess I'll wait on you, sugar." She reverted to English. "And hope I helped you work up an appetite... after last night."

"You sure did, angel." Grinning, he sat up, pushed himself to the edge of the bed. "Alright. I'm coming."

"Again?" Her grin was teasing.

"Later, you cheeky minx."

Anyone listening in would never imagine that the two of them were anything other than lovers entirely comfortable in each other's company, Pascal thought as he headed for the bathroom. It felt so easy, so natural, to banter with Jess. He couldn't help but think how much he wanted to do it without having to be mindful that every word out of both their mouths was being listened to by people who would kill them without a second thought if they found out who he and Jess really were.

“Time to get down to business,” he whispered to himself in the mirror as he washed his face. “Stay sharp.”

He dressed in loose tan cotton pants and a white shirt open at the neck, deck shoes on his feet. Everything was French in origin, as was almost everything else in his suitcase, in keeping with his cover. Pascal Montalban projected himself as a man simple in tastes, ruthless in pursuit of a deal. Jess didn’t quite fit, in truth, but he was banking on the fact that Fortuna didn’t know him personally and might not realize that, and that Dzokharov and Yoon, both of whom *did* know him, wouldn’t care enough to comment.

Besides, Jess was the kind of woman who could make any man rethink his tastes and priorities.

They walked down to the main building together. Jess had donned her Cartier sunglasses and a big floppy hat, loudly declaiming as they walked through the pool area that her tan came from a spray booth, thank you kindly, she didn’t fancy skin cancer. Two girls already sunning themselves by the pool both looked askance at her.

"Play nice, Jess," Pascal reproached. "Make friends with the other girls. You'll be bored if you alienate them all and have nobody to talk to."

She sighed exaggeratedly, and he was sure she was rolling her eyes behind her sunglasses. "I guess. Since you *confiscated* my *phone*. Nobody's done that to me since I was in prep school."

"Girls and their phones." Dieter Breukel, the Dutchman, overheard her remark as they walked into the dining room and turned to face them, shaking his head. "Let me guess. Instagram?"

"Do you recognize me?" Jess preened. "I mean, I'm not *super* famous. I've only got six hundred thousand followers."

Breukel's look at Pascal was frankly commiserating, and he stopped trying to restrain his laughter, though it wasn't for the reason Breukel probably assumed. Jess was one hell of an actress.

"What's for breakfast?" Jess cast Breukel a sunny smile and walked over to the buffet set out at the side of the room. "There'd better be decent tea. Oh, an egg chef! Do you have Hollandaise sauce? I'd love an eggs Benedict."

"Stunning," Breukel murmured to Pascal as Jess swanned off, "but too high maintenance for my tastes."

"I thought she might be for mine at first, but I'm finding her worth the effort," Pascal responded.

"You're not afraid she might be seen as a weak spot for you?"

Well, that was direct. Pascal turned to make direct eye contact with the other man, wondering what Breukel's game was. "Anyone who tried to exploit Jess to get at me in any way would soon discover they had made a fatal mistake," he said, his voice quite toneless.

Breukel inclined his head, glanced at Jess again, brow furrowing, and said nothing more, just helping himself to toast, bacon and grilled tomatoes before sitting down and signaling a waiter to pour him coffee.

There was nobody else at breakfast apart from the staff. Jessikah made an effort at polite conversation, not chattering at Breukel but trying to involve him. He responded monosyllabically to her efforts, and eventually she gave up, shrugging expressively at Pascal. He patted her hand consolingly.

“So where is everyone else?” Jess asked after they ate in silence for a few minutes.

“A late night, I think,” Breukel said.

“Not you?” Pascal asked.

“I left the party around two. I could have done with a little more sleep, but the jet lag had me awake just after dawn.” Breukel’s smile was tight. “Yesterday was a long travel day.”

“See, I don’t want to hear any more of your whining about the travel efforts,” Pascal noted to Jess. “At least we didn’t have to come from Europe!”

“Or North Korea.” Breukel lowered his voice slightly, nodding towards the door, and Pascal saw Mr Yoon entering the room, one of Fortuna’s girls clinging to his arm, and his translator following behind, her eyes cast down.

"Lordy," Jessikah murmured, "I wonder if she had to translate for him while he was in bed with that other girl? Poor girl, what a shit job."

Breukel snorted with laughter, covering his mouth with his napkin, and glanced at Pascal. "I begin to see why you think she's worth the effort," he murmured. "Girl's funny."

"And smart." Pascal put on a fondly proud expression. "Even if she can be a bit of a bitch on occasion."

"What was bitchy about feeling sorry for the poor girl?" Jess said indignantly.

"All right, all right." He put a hand on her arm in a soothing gesture. "You can be nice."

"*Very* nice." She cast him a sideways look under her lashes.

"When you want to be."

She sniffed and returned her attention to her breakfast.

Yoon and the two women with him sat down at the other end of the long table, though the translator cast a quick, almost wistful glance in their direction, as though she would far rather be sitting anywhere else but with her boss and his new paramour.

"I'm done," Jess said quietly after a little while. "What now? Do we just wait around for Mr Fortuna?"

"I will. You go enjoy yourself. Meet the other girls, relax by the pool." He pulled her in for a kiss. "Don't stray off." He punctuated that last comment with a meaningful look.

"I won't. I promise." She squeezed his hand lightly. "No wandering around unless you're with me."

"Good girl." He kissed her again, patted her ass as she stood up.

Jess cast him a mock-indignant look, but she also threw some extra sashay into her hips as she walked out, making him chuckle quietly under his breath. Breukel turned to watch her go, and even Yoon dropped his hand from the local girl's thigh and stared.

"Good mornin', Mr Fortuna." Pascal stiffened as he heard Jess's voice float back to them from just outside the dining room.

“Good morning, my dear. Did you sleep well? And I hope you enjoyed your breakfast?”

“Yes to both, thank you very much. And now I’m off to enjoy some more of your hospitality with a swim in that beautiful pool. Enjoy *your* breakfast!”

Fortuna was looking over his shoulder as he left the room, obviously appreciating the back view of Jess walking away… even though he had a beautiful girl on each arm. Turning around, he caught Pascal’s eye and grinned unrepentantly.

“No laws against window shopping,” he said flippantly.

“Yeah. Just rude to handle other folks’ property when it’s not for sale,” Pascal said, putting a gentle hint of menace in his tone.

“Oh, I’ve got my hands full already.” Fortuna laughed easily, squeezing the waists of the women on either side of him. “I see we’re almost all here. Just the general and Mr Hayworth to come.”

“Hayworth seems an odd duck.” Pascal decided to push a little. It was natural to be curious, after all. "I'd never heard of him, but Jess says his father's some sort of fundamentalist preacher."

"Seems the case," Fortuna agreed easily, taking a seat after ordering one of the girls with him to fetch him some breakfast.

"A doomsday cult kind of thing?" Breukel asked, obviously curious too. "I'd never heard of him either," he said when Pascal glanced his way. "And let's be honest; people usually don't come straight to this end of the market. Where and what has he been buying up to this point, and who with?"

"Yeah," Pascal agreed. "I know everyone else here by reputation even if I haven't met them in person before. Hayworth is a blank slate, and I don't like those. How do you know he's for real and not a plant, Fortuna?"

"The same way I know you are both for real," Fortuna said, a little coldly. "I do my homework. Hayworth is a genuine buyer, and he's probably got more cash on hand than either of the buyers you two are here representing. Who you'll note, I'm not pressing you to tell me about because *I* understand how discretion works in our business."

Pascal ducked his head, doing his best to look chastened. Breukel grunted a noise that might have been an apology.

"You and I haven't met before," Fortuna said directly to Pascal, "but we've been dealing indirectly for years, and we have clients in common, have ended up as middlemen in the same deals more than once. I know you're legit, and Dieter and I have dealt directly together in the past. You're both just going to have to trust me."

"Trust doesn't come all that easy in this business," Pascal said, an oblique apology, "and we're already putting a whole lot of trust in you. We're on your private island, cut off from all communications, no way for another soul to know where we are… or what could have happened to us if we don't reappear on the grid again at some point. Not to mention the magnitude of the deal we're doing here; let's not kid ourselves, this is pretty extreme even in our line of work. I don't know how Breukel feels, but it makes *me* feel pretty damn jumpy when there's a guy here whose presence doesn't seem to make any sense."

Fortuna sighed. "I do see where you're coming from. As you say, this is quite some deal. The terms are set, however. All the bidders have been vetted. Frankly, you're lucky I allowed you two in here rather than insisting your clients reveal themselves and attend in person; it's only your reputations that got you in the door."

"And our hefty deposits, of course," Breukel said dryly.

"Of course. You did win the online preliminary auctions." Fortuna's smile was sly. "Nevertheless, if you hadn't passed my background checks, you wouldn't be here. And neither would Hayworth, so as long as you're planning to stay for the final auctions, I don't want to hear any more about it."

"Fair enough," Pascal said finally, with a shrug. "You've probably got more to lose than I have. And *he's* probably got more to lose than either of us." He nodded to where Hayworth was coming in the door, alone.

“Good morning, Saul!” Fortuna cast Pascal a warning look before waving Hayworth over. “Where’s Camila? Did she not please you?”

“Sure, she did,” Hayworth said. “She’s still sleepin’ it off. I might have been a little rough on her.”

Pascal didn’t like the sound of that. And he was definitely glad Jess wasn’t present, because she’d probably have arced up and stormed off to check on Camila’s welfare.

“Takes a real man to beat the shit out a woman in bed,” he murmured in an undertone to Breukel as Hayworth walked away to help himself to the buffet. “Fucking evangelical types. They’re always compensating for something.”

Breukel laughed, and Fortuna snickered too.

“So.” Pascal raised his voice back to normal levels, leaned back in his chair with his coffee cup in hand. “When do we get down to business?”

“Just relax and enjoy today,” Fortuna gave him a non-answer. “I need to wait for some pieces to be in place. Should have word by tonight.”

"Fair enough. You told us to expect to be here for a few days. It's been a while since I had an actual holiday, and that pool of yours does look pretty inviting."

"As do the girls," Breukel noted. "I was too jet-lagged last night, but..."

Fortuna laughed expansively, clapped him on the back. "You'll find them very accommodating, I promise you, my friend! Enjoy my hospitality, and tomorrow we'll get down to business."

Chapter 11

There were five girls in the group by the pool now, and one of them was in tears and had fresh, purpling bruises around her wrists and a black eye. It wasn't Mariska, the young Chechen, either. Mariska was trying to comfort the crying girl, whose rippling dark hair and copper-gold skin suggested she was a local.

"Oh my God." Jess stalked straight over, indignation bubbling up inside her. "Who did this to you? Was it Dzhokharov?" she demanded of Mariska.

The Chechen girl shook her head. "He not hit. Frighten other ways." She grimaced.

"Bad enough." Jess crouched down in front of the crying girl. "Let me look, sugar." She tried to make her voice gentle, despite her anger. "What's your name?"

"C-Camila," the crying girl hiccuped. "The American. The preacher. I thought... thought a God-fearing man would never..."

"They are the worse kind," one of the other girls muttered. "All the words are false."

"Is just bruises." Camila pulled her hands away from Jess when she tried to look at the marks on her wrists. "They heal."

"You better go back to our villa," the other girl said. "Baz not like us to be seen not looking our best."

"Yeah, I go. Good luck whoever gets him next." Camila sniffled and wiped at her eyes.

The other girls looked at each other with open dread.

"Maybe we could draw straws?" one of them said. Or that was what Jess thought she said, because she'd spoken Spanish, and Jess's Spanish wasn't nearly as good as her French. She was pretty sure she was getting the gist of the conversation, though Mariska was looking blank.

"You know that's not how it works. They point and we go. We're being well paid enough. I won't earn this kind of money in six months back in Caracas. As long as there are no broken bones, well." The girl who was speaking, a stunner with deep brown skin and mahogany-highlighted black hair, shrugged. "I've had bruises. They don't show up so much on me. I'll take the preacher for a night. Maybe teach him a thing or two."

"Good luck with that, Soraya," Camila said cynically, before shrugging and getting to her feet. "Thanks," she said in English to Mariska and Jess. "You're kind. Thank you."

"You're welcome, honey. You sure you're gonna be okay?" Jess asked. "If you need any help..."

"I'll be okay." Camila nodded and walked away, moving slowly and stiffly.

"What a bastard," Jess muttered. "Can't stand men who beat up on women. Scum."

"You don't have to worry. You came with your man, you don't have to go with whoever points," Soraya said, her tone dismissive.

"And that means I shouldn't care about the rest of you? Well, I do!" Jess said indignantly.

Soraya curled her lip cynically, but the other girls were looking at Jess with small smiles and open expressions.

Allies, Jess thought, and if the girls were kindly disposed to her, maybe they'd be less likely to tell if they saw her doing something which might otherwise be considered suspicious.

"How old are you anyway?" she asked Mariska.

"Fifteen," Mariska said, and several of the other girls gasped aloud.

"... next month," Mariska added.

"*Cabronazo*," one of the other girls said, clearly disgusted.

Jess had no idea what that meant, but she had a pretty fair idea. She felt more than slightly queasy. *I'm twice this child's age. I have to get her out of here.*

But the mission had to come first. Pascal was right about that. Too many lives were at stake.

Mariska seemed to shrink into herself, looking past Jess, and Jess turned to see Dzhokharov walking through the pool area, another girl on his arm. He didn't even seem to see Mariska there.

"At least we can give you a break from him for a few days," Soraya said, her tone much more kindly, and Mariska gave her a small, grateful smile.

"He's not so bad," she murmured. "Not rough."

But he likes fourteen-year-old girls, Jess thought, and had to bite hard on her tongue.

As the girls settled into the lounge chairs around the pool, she made sure she took one close to Mariska, both of them choosing seats in the shade - Jess hadn't been joking about her tan coming from a spray booth. She didn't want to burn, and Mariska, with her pale European skin, would burn even more easily.

"How long have you been with Dzhokharov?" she asked quietly.

"A few months." Mariska's expression was placid. "My father sold me to him when he passed through our village and saw me."

Jess choked. "Your father... sold you?"

"It is not so uncommon, in Chechnya. My mother would be angry, but she died two years. I have older sisters, they cook and clean for my father, but I am the pretty one. The general wanted me. He paid my father much money."

Mariska was unquestionably beautiful, not merely pretty. Tawny bronze hair with streaks of gold, a high-cheekboned face with a delicately pointed chin and bright, grass-green eyes, a petite figure and an almost fragile air about her.

"My father's rich," Jess said. "Rich enough to make sure if you didn't want to be found, you wouldn't be. Buy you a new identity. When we get out of here, I want you to find a way to get away from Dzhokharov and contact me."

"Why would you do that? You don't know me." Mariska looked wary.

“I know I don’t like men who buy fourteen-year-old girls, and that’s all I need to know. I’m serious, Mariska. You could have a whole new life, in America. I’ll help you.”

“You are kind person.” Mariska’s face softened. “I believe you.”

“I don’t have my phone, and I’m sure you don’t either, but can you remember an email?” Jess rattled off one of her many anonymous email addresses, making a mental note to put an alert on it for anything incoming which might potentially be from Mariska.

“I remember.” Mariska repeated it back. “If he ever bring me to America, I find a way.”

“Find a way no matter where you are. I told you. My father’s rich. I can get you new documents, a new passport. He’d never even know where to start looking.”

Another woman came out to join them then, the Korean translator attending Mr Yoon. She paused, looking at the women lounging by the pool, looked at the water. A tiny, slender woman, she was dressed quite unsuitably for the climate, in a plainly tailored navy skirt suit and high-collared white blouse.

“Don’t you have a swimsuit?” Soraya said, her tone cutting. “I’d lend you one, but I don’t think it’d fit.” The Venezuelan beauty looked down at her magnificent chest with a satisfied smirk.

“Oh no, thank you,” the Korean woman said in clipped, accentless English. “I wouldn’t want to look like a slut anyway.” She turned and walked away in her sensible flat shoes, leaving Soraya gaping and Jess choking back a laugh. Slut-shaming wasn’t nice, but Soraya had started that.

The men started coming out then, Pascal coming over and sitting on the end of Jess’s chair. She greeted him with a kiss, half her attention on watching where the others were going. Yoon followed after his translator, probably heading back to his villa, but the other men found seats. Soraya, as good as her word to Camila, got up from her chair and went over to Hayworth, draping herself languidly over the chair beside him and obviously flirting hard. Hayworth seemed to take the bait, gaze glued to Soraya’s breasts overflowing her red string bikini.

“So, what’s the plan for today?” Jess murmured, resting her chin on Pascal’s shoulder.

“The plan is that there is no plan. Fortuna says some pieces aren’t in place yet. Business tomorrow, leisure today.”

Their eyes met, and Jess swallowed down frustration. Still, more time to scout about, maybe figure out where the door to get into the server room was, would definitely be welcome.

“Sounds lovely. I think I’m going to have a swim,” she said. “You coming in?” They could cuddle and murmur sweet nothings - at least, that’s what any observer would think they were doing - but even the most sensitive microphone would never be able to distinguish their words over the splashing of the water.

“Sure thing.”

They both stripped down to their swimsuits and slipped into the water; nobody else joined them yet, sitting around talking and sipping on fruit juice or coffee... or champagne, as Josef brought out a bottle and began to fill glasses.

Get everyone drunk early and keep them entertained, Jess thought. *Not the worst plan*. Wealthy, powerful men didn't like to be kept waiting. She suspected Fortuna was more irritated than he was showing, that he wasn't able to conduct his first auction yet.

"So what have you found out?" Pascal murmured, nuzzling her neck.

"Hayworth likes to beat up women and Mariska's fourteen," she whispered back.

"Holy shit." Pascal stiffened, then obviously made himself relax, huffing out a breath. "Jess..."

"I know. Not why we're here. But this is relevant; none of the girls have any sort of loyalty to Fortuna. They're being well paid - Soraya, the girl who's talking to Hayworth, said she would take six months to earn as much back in Caracas. And look at her. A girl that beautiful would be expensive anywhere."

"Hm." Pascal nibbled on Jess's earlobe, and goosebumps ran the length of her spine. "They're all sex workers?"

"Yes. Camila - the girl Hayworth beat up - said if the men point, they have to go."

"So there's no ideology driving them to report anything they see out of the ordinary."

"Nor likely to make them suspicious. And Mariska clearly hates Dzhokharov; the only woman I'd be concerned about is Yoon's translator. Do we even know her name?"

"He certainly hasn't introduced her. Treats her like a robot. She'll share his ideology though, so watch out around her."

"Are you two swimming, or just necking?" It was Breukel, the Dutchman, who interrupted, finally joining them in the pool. "Because if the latter, interested in a third?" He leered at Jess, but oddly enough, she didn't feel threatened by him.

"Pascal is more than enough man for me." Jess tucked her head under Pascal's chin, smiling at Breukel. "Come on. Plenty of beautiful girls here who'd be delighted to keep you company."

"Yes, but only one of them has managed to make me laugh so far." Breukel sighed, but he was grinning and appeared entirely unoffended by her refusal. "Ah well. Can't blame a man for trying."

"Only for trying again, after he's already been turned down." Pascal's tone was warning.

"Don't worry about me, Montalban. I know what *no* means. Unlike some." Breukel's glance in Fortuna's direction was meaningful.

That was... interesting. And slightly concerning. Was Breukel warning them that Fortuna had said something about continuing to pursue Jess, even after Pascal had warned him off? And what would Breukel's motives be for doing that?

Jess pulled her head back and met Pascal's gaze, seeing her queries mirrored there.

"Has Breukel given any hints who his clients might be?" she asked quietly, at the first opportunity once the Dutchman had moved away.

"No. And I'm starting to wonder if he might not have similar clients to us," Pascal murmured.

"Like..."

"Interpol," he barely breathed the word. "But we can't know for sure. So don't let your guard down, because if we're wrong, we're both dead."

"Understood."

"And now we'd better get out of this pool. I think you're starting to wrinkle." His grin was teasing.

"You." She pinched lightly at his ribs. Well. Tried to. He was so muscled and lean she could barely get any loose skin to pinch.

Pascal just laughed, his hands closing around her waist and lifting her up. She hooked her legs around his waist instinctively, and he carried her to the edge of the pool and lifted her up out of the water.

Jess certainly wasn't innocent, and Pascal was far from the first man she'd been intimate with, but looking into his amber-gold eyes, she honestly couldn't recall ever having such a close connection with anyone. Despite their very different backgrounds, even the age gap between them, they seemed to be on the same wavelength. And the attraction she felt for him was undeniable. Impulsively, she leaned down, slanting her mouth over his.

She'd half expected him to tense, pull away, despite their audience. He didn't. He kissed her back, his fingers tightening on her waist, digging in lightly.

It was ridiculous for her to tremble in his arms like a teenage girl being kissed for the first time, but she couldn't stop the shiver that raced down her spine.

When she got out of the pool, an entirely different prickle raced down her spine and she knew, without looking at him, that Baz Fortuna was watching her, eyes tracing greedily over her body. She made herself move slowly, casually, back to her chair and pick up the towel draped over it. Every instinct was screaming at her to wrap herself up in it, conceal her from his gaze, but it would make him suspicious. Instead she dried herself off with casual pats, tossed the towel back down on the chair and draped herself languorously over it.

“No phone, so I can’t even listen to my tunes. Don’t you even have a CD player? Or a record player or something, since everything’s so analog here?” She curled her lip in Fortuna’s direction.

“We can arrange some music.” He flicked a finger at Josef, who jumped to attention. “Any requests, Jessica?”

She slid her sunglasses down her nose, peered at him over them. “No offense. But you’re kinda old. Don’t think you’re likely to have much that aligns with my taste in music.”

From the corner of her eye she saw Pascal turn away, clearly stifling a laugh. Breukel snickered, Dzhokharov let out a roar of laughter, and Fortuna looked offended, though she could tell he was trying to hide it. *He’s been too long out of the CIA,* Jess thought. *He’s forgotten his poker face, and he’s way too used to everyone being sycophantic. Especially women.*

“You don’t know your place, woman. Be quiet, or your mouth will be closed for you.”

Startled, she snapped her head around to stare at the speaker; Saul Hayworth, the preacher's son. The cultist. She was just opening her mouth to be rude to him as well when Pascal stepped in between them.

"If you speak to her again, I will tear your dick off with my bare hands and make you eat it." His tone was pure menace as he loomed over the smaller, slighter man, and Hayworth cringed back instinctively from the danger Pascal exuded, before obviously remembering his own perceived power. He opened his mouth again, but Pascal moved closer, leaning down to get right in his face.

"I don't give a fuck who you are, or who your daddy is, or how much money you've got. You threaten my woman, you'll answer to me."

"Gentlemen." Fortuna was on his feet, moving in between them quickly, though Jess noticed he didn't actually touch Pascal, just holding his hand up towards him and gesturing him to move back. "That's enough. Saul, I took no insult; Jess amuses me. But I cannot have threats made against other guests."

“Reprimand him, then!” Hayworth was shaking, with fear or rage or perhaps a combination of both.

“You made the first threat,” Fortuna said gently. “Jess is also my guest.”

“A woman…”

“A *guest*.”

The two stared at each other, briefly at loggerheads, before Hayworth shrugged ungraciously. “Whatever.” He cast a sideways glance full of bitterness at Jess, though, and she had the sudden sinking feeling she’d made matters much worse for whatever poor woman he chose for his bed next, however unintentionally. Maybe Camila had been the lucky one, after all.

Chapter 12

The day passed in a weird combination of boredom and steadily increasing tension. Hayworth had stomped off, muttering that he was going to his villa. Fortuna pointed at Soraya and gestured after him; the girl got up with a sigh and left.

"He beat up one of your other girls," Jess told Fortuna, obviously unable to keep her mouth shut. "I don't think you're paying them enough to put up with that shit."

Fortuna looked at her thoughtfully. "You're a brave young woman, Jess. I'll take what you just said into consideration." He wagged a finger at her. "But you do need to learn when to keep your mouth shut. In my and Pascal's line of work... you'll meet a lot of men with big egos. Some of whom won't hesitate to carry out threats."

She nodded, as though carefully considering what he'd said. "I get it." Ducking her head, as though bashful, she added "I just get mad when I see people being cruel for no reason."

"You're very young." It didn't sound like a compliment. Fortuna nodded at Pascal. "She'll get over it. Or she won't."

He knew what the other man meant. Either Jess would harden up enough to survive as an arms dealer's girlfriend, or she wouldn't, and Pascal would decide she wasn't worth the trouble.

Josef had put on some music, piped out through speakers on the side of the cabana beside the pool, and Jess was wise enough not to comment on the playlist.

Waitstaff brought out platters of food and more bottles of champagne at lunchtime, and most of the party got steadily more tipsy. Pascal and Jess both drank judiciously; he saw her pour quite a bit surreptitiously into the lush palm foliage around them, mostly using his broad back for cover.

Dzhokharov got particularly loud and boisterous, though fortunately he ignored Mariska in favor of Adelie, another of Fortuna's lovely local girls, and eventually took her off to his villa mid-afternoon.

"We can sneak off for a while too. Won't look unusual," Jess murmured in Pascal's ear, and he nodded. Nobody was paying attention to them anyway. Breukel was asleep on a deck chair, obviously still affected by jet lag, and Yoon and Fortuna were playing chess, lack of a language in common no barrier in the ancient game. Josef and two other men sat at a table not far away, drinking and talking.

"It's cooling down now. Let's go for a walk on the beach before we go shower and change for dinner," Pascal suggested at normal volume, and Fortuna didn't even glance up, just lifted a hand in acknowledgment.

They'd be able to actually talk without fear of being overheard, and Pascal felt the tension start to leave him almost as soon as they were out of earshot of the crowd around the pool.

"How do you do this for months on end?" Jess muttered, rolling her shoulders as if she, too, was feeling the tension. “Watch every word out of your mouth?”

“You get used to it. You’re going great. I honestly can’t tell what’s really you and what’s your persona. She’s very authentic.”

“Well.” She shot him a weary little sideways smile. “She’s pretty heavily based on me. A few years younger, a lot more sheltered, but just as prone to speaking her mind without thought for the consequences.”

“It’s clever. At first I thought you were putting yourself on Fortuna’s radar too much, but I’ve changed my mind… he’s dismissed you as naive and more hassle than you’re worth.”

Jess grinned. “That’s what I was aiming for. After last night, I figured he was a bit too attentive. Thought I’d show him how annoying a girl with an opinion can be. He’s an arrogant bastard. The last thing he wants is someone who’ll talk back to him all the time.”

“You’re not just hacker-smart, are you?” They were in full view of windows of some of the private villas, so he slung his arm around her shoulders and hugged her close.

"You thought I was a tech nerd with no real world experience, huh?" She fluttered her eyelashes at him. "You're not wholly wrong, if I'm being honest with you, and I think we have to be honest with each other. I'm totally making it up as I go along, but I've always believed I have good instincts."

"You do." He hesitated, then gave her complete honesty in return. "I never doubted your technical skills, but this part of it?" He gestured around with his free hand, indicating their surrounds, the island, the whole situation. "This gave me pause. But I'm impressed. If it wasn't more than obvious that you're doing very nicely working for yourself, I'd be trying very hard to recruit you for the Agency."

She threw back her head and laughed, leaning into him. "Funny. I've been thinking the same thing."

"What?" Startled, he stopped walking. "You... want to try and recruit *me*?"

"We work well together, don't you think? I could pay you a lot better. And you wouldn't have to live undercover like you do now."

He was so stunned he didn't know what to say, despite Drew Murphy having hinted about exactly this when they talked at Hestia Global's headquarters just a few days ago. Eventually, he started walking again, and Jess kept pace, syncing her stride perfectly with his.

"What I do is important," he said finally.

"Of course it is. And if we pull this one off - *when* we pull this one off, let's think positive - the lives saved will be literally incalculable. But at the same time, Pascal," she peered up at him. "What do you think our odds of pulling it off without your cover getting burned are?"

Once again, she managed to stun him into silence, because he *hadn't* thought about it. Hadn't thought beyond stopping those nukes falling into the wrong hands.

Jess was right, though. If they were successful here, all the buyers and Fortuna and his men would all go to prison. Guantanamo, most likely; it was close, and the CIA would decide what to do with each of them from there, but Yoon and Dzhokharov at least would probably be traded back to their respective nations in some sort of quid pro quo deal sooner rather than later. And that meant Pascal Montalban couldn't reappear ever again, because both men would know that he was supposed to be locked up with the key thrown away.

Assuming he didn't have to completely blow his cover to get the mission done anyway.

"Shit," he muttered under his breath, realizing how it was going to play out. If they succeeded, he'd be a hero within the Agency, of course, but they would have no choice but to take him out of the field permanently. He'd be promoted to a desk job.

But... he followed the line of thinking to the logical conclusion. He couldn't ever be promoted all that high. Never to a point of public visibility, because too many underworld types knew his face. Yoon and Dzhokharov would put him on their respective governments' hit lists if they ever knew he wasn't dead or in jail.

"Think about it," Jess said finally, breaking the silence that had fallen between them as he thought. "The offer's open, whenever you're ready, however it plays out with your bosses when this is all over. You know where to find me. I'll beat whatever offer the Agency makes you... and I promise, you won't have to be chained to a desk."

"I'll think about it. *If* we make it through this," he said, his tone a warning. "We've a long way to go."

"Talking of which." Her irrepressible grin reappeared, dimples flashing in her cheeks. "What say you authorize me doing a bit of sneaking around tonight? I want to figure out how to get into that server room. Your boss must be going mad by now, and Liane will be worrying about me."

"You got a plan?" He had a few ideas himself, but he wanted to hear hers. She was clearly damn smart, with good tactical instincts, and he'd be stupid not to make use of her brain as the asset it was.

"Some sort of diversion. Fortuna will probably encourage another party tonight - he's lazy - which will keep the guests occupied, but we want something to interest his men as well."

"Please don't suggest you're going to put on a strip show."

She pinched his arm. "Wouldn't be much use if I want to be the one sneaking around, would it? I was thinking card games. Blackjack to start. Maybe some high-stakes poker after. Even if the guards aren't invited to play at the tables, they'll get sucked in to watching."

"Brilliant," he murmured. "And you..?"

"I'll play for the first part of the evening. Deal some blackjack, maybe be a bit showy about it. Then claim I'm tired because you've been busy screwing my brains out, and go to bed... except I'll immediately sneak back out again."

He didn't like it. "If you're caught..."

"You disavow me." Her gaze was clear-eyed, calm. "Claim you've been taken in by a honey trap agent. Do what you have to do."

"He'll want me to kill you. I can't do that, Jess. You don't understand how deep we're in, here."

She hesitated, and then shrugged, her jaw setting stubbornly. "I'd better not get caught, then."

"Jess..."

"Do you have a better plan?"

He didn't, and he didn't like it. Fortuna's men were going to be watching the buyers, watching *him*, far more closely than they would Jess. Untrained in spycraft as she was, she still had to be the one to do this, because once they found the server room, she was the one who had to go in anyway. Going twice, once for him to find the way and once for her to go in, doubled the risk.

"All right," he said quietly at last. "We'll do it your way. But don't take any risks you don't have to, and if you're caught... kill whoever catches you."

It was Jess's turn to freeze with shock. "What?"

"It's you or them. If they catch you sneaking around and drag you in front of Fortuna, you're dead. I can't see you running into more than one or two guards. Catch them by surprise and you can do it."

"With *what*?"

"Make it look like they got in a fight and killed each other, if there are two of them."

He blinked at the look she was giving him. "What?"

"How many people have you killed, that you're so casual about it?"

It was a question he didn't want to answer. Didn't even know how to answer. "I was a Ranger before I ever joined the Agency," he said finally. "We kill. We're good at it."

He didn't have to ask whether she'd ever fired a weapon in anger when she worked for the NSA. She'd spent her time there behind the safety of a computer screen, it was obvious. But he wasn't going to insult her by asking if she could do it. She understood the stakes now.

"Come on." She took his hand. "We need to go back and put on another audio show of having loud and enthusiastic sex, and then get ready for dinner. Wait until you see the dress I'm gonna wear. I told the other girls about it too, and saw a competitive glint light up more than a few eyes, so they'll all be pulling out all the stops as well."

"Making sure all the guards are as distracted as possible," Pascal murmured, shaking his head. “You sure as hell think fast on your feet, Jess.”

“I hope so.” She grinned.

“You’re gonna do great.” He tried to project a confidence he wasn’t quite feeling. It was going to eat him up inside, forced to sit at a table and play poker while she crept around in the dark doing the actual important work of the mission, but this was the part only she could do, and he well knew it.

The dress she put on was quite simply incredible; an aqua-green, shimmering scrap of silk with no back and a deeply swooping neckline in the front. He watched in sheer amazement as she used double-sided tape to stick it to the sides of her breasts, grinning over her shoulder at him.

“What, you’ve never watched a woman tape herself into her dress so she doesn’t accidentally flash everyone before?”

“An entirely new experience for me,” Pascal admitted, reclining on the bed and watching in unconcealed fascination.

She laughed, picking up a lip pencil. “Stick with me, buddy. I’ll open your eyes to a whole world of new experiences.”

“You already are. Wouldn’t have missed this for anything. Never had such a good view.”

Jess turned, lip pencil in hand, and raised an elegant eyebrow at him. “You do say some real sweet things, sugar. Reminds me why I took up with you in the first place.”

“Just the things I *say*?” Getting off the bed, he walked over to her.

“Oh. A few other things too. The jewelry’s nice.” She fingered the diamond hanging on a gold chain at her throat… one he really hoped hadn’t been bought with his credit card, but there was a laughing twinkle in her eyes.

“Hellion,” he murmured.

“Oh, you know it.” She chuckled and turned back to the mirror, leaning in close to outline her lips. “You’re going to owe me some earrings at least to go with these when we get home, after making me suffer without my phone for however long we’re stuck here. That tennis bracelet, too.”

"You'll have earned both." He meant every word, and he'd buy them for her himself.

If they got home.

Chapter 13

Every eye turned to Jess when they walked into the main lounge, just as she'd planned. Dzhokharov, obviously even drunker than he'd been earlier in the afternoon, whistled coarsely.

"Stunning, Jess." Fortuna came up to her, swept her hand up and kissed it extravagantly. "I appreciate you making the effort, for such a small audience... can't even post to your Instagram account!"

"Well, if you checked out my Insta, you'll know I don't actually post many photos of myself," Jess said pertly.

"Which is a shame, because you really are so very photogenic." Fortuna gave his genial smile, the one that never quite reached his eyes.

"So what's the plan for this evening?" she asked brightly, smiling at Breukel. "Something fun, I hope!"

It only took one whisper of the word *cards*, carefully done while Fortuna was talking to Yoon and his translator, and Dzhokharov jumped on it. Soon the Chechen was all but demanding they play, and if anyone asked him afterwards, he'd probably be convinced it was all his own idea.

"I can deal blackjack," Jess said brightly, "would you like me to? Do you have a few packs of cards around somewhere, Baz?"

"I'm sure we can rustle some up." Fortuna snapped his fingers at Josef, who disappeared for a few minutes and eventually returned with three fairly well-thumbed packs of cards. Guard entertainment, Jess guessed, taking the packs from Josef.

"Best stay here to play, hm?" She deftly started shuffling the cards together. "Not a decent size table in the lounge." And with the door closed, nobody could possibly look through the window to the other side of that alley and see her sneaking into the server room.

"No dealing off the bottom of the deck, now." Fortuna settled into the seat directly opposite her, smirking. "I'm watching you."

"I wouldn't dare," she said demurely.

"But what are we gambling for? I did not bring cash, and without phones, we cannot transfer assets," Yoon's translator said, standing at her boss's shoulder as he took his seat.

"Counters. We'll agree in advance what they are worth. Josef." Fortuna snapped his fingers again. "Find something. We'll play a few practice hands while you do. Just so I can see how Jess deals."

The long-suffering aide actually rolled his eyes behind his boss's back, but took off again. He eventually returned with some obviously hastily-printed and cut paper tokens, each with 100 printed on them.

"That'll do. To start with." Fortuna took the stack, eyed Josef. "Get more."

"Sir."

Jess wished she could follow, to where there was obviously a computer and printer, but all she could do was sit there and draw cards. Best to wait anyway, she consoled herself. She could hardly break into the server room while Josef was in there printing off gambling tokens!

It was interesting, watching the different strategies the men employed playing blackjack. Pascal, Fortuna and Breukel both had very similar strategies, very conventional in style. Yoon was extremely cautious, though more familiar with the game than she might have expected. Hayworth was absolutely reckless, and Dzhokharov, despite his drunkenness, was actually a very good player. The Chechen was soon amassing quite a little stack of tokens in front of him.

Hayworth, true to form, soon began to get annoyed at his poor play and started muttering under his breath that Jess must be cheating somehow.

“She isn’t,” Fortuna said shortly. “Trust me, I’d know. She’s being very careful to only slide cards from the top of the deck, and sure as hell there's nowhere to hide any cards in that outfit."

There was laughter around the table. Jess flipped a card in front of Hayworth.

"Without being rude, Mr Hayworth, have you played this game much?"

He hesitated for a beat, then shook his head. "Can't be seen doing this kind of thing in public, you understand."

"Of course," she said understandingly. "Of course you have the basic rules down, but there are a few simple strategies you really should understand too. See here... you've got seventeen. What do you think you should do?"

"Well he's got eighteen, so I have to hit." Hayworth pointed to Breukel's cards.

Breukel snorted, then said in rapid French, "What an absolute idiot."

Pascal, Fortuna, and a little surprisingly, Dzhokharov, all laughed, hiding it with various degrees of effort, which was to say in Dzhokharov's case not at all. Jess tried to ignore them all.

"You're not playing *them*, Mr Hayworth. The only card you have to worry about is the one in front of the dealer. Which is a six, see? So you're actually in a really good position. I have to draw until I hit seventeen at least, which means there's a good chance this hand will be a bust."

"Oh." He stared at the six in front of her, then at the hands of the other men. "So I don't need to bother about what they have?"

"Not in blackjack. You're only playing the house. Now if they start playing poker later, you might be in more trouble." She gave him a gentle smile. Flipped another card over and made a face. "Oh dear. A queen. That puts me on sixteen... not many options for me to win against you."

Hayworth looked quite eager. Jess smiled at him and flipped over another six. "Bust."

"Yeah!" Hayworth pumped his fist as Jess slid tokens in his direction.

"Let me help you out. I play this game good." Soraya, the beauty who'd gone off with Hayworth earlier and returned without bruises, slinked up behind him, and he pulled her onto his lap.

"That's it. I need a good luck charm."

Fortuna caught Jess's eye, tilted his head towards Hayworth, and mouthed something she couldn't quite understand. She frowned, puzzled.

"Give him good cards."

She made out the words this time. Looked down at her hands and thought fast. Then looked back up at Fortuna and made a helpless face. "I can't," she mouthed.

Admitting to being able to cheat might raise his suspicions of her again, and she wanted him to keep thinking of her as a mouthy, naive type with not that much real world experience.

Fortuna gave her a benign little smile and nodded, accepting the answer. Turned to wave Josef over with more tokens.

They played for another hour, and then Jess started to fumble a little, yawn a few times behind her hand. When she dropped half the cards while shuffling them and had to gather them awkwardly, Pascal said “Are you tired, Jess?”

“I’m afraid so.” She smiled at him, lowering her lashes a little bashfully. “I think you’ve worn me out.”

There were some crude laughs around the table, and she let a blush come to her cheeks, keeping her eyes downcast.

“Go to bed, angel,” Pascal said. “I’ll wake you when I get back.”

“All right. Maybe one of the other girls can deal for you. Soraya?”

“I can do it,” the Venezuelan beauty said easily. “Saul understands better now, I think.”

“Gettin’ by.” He’d played as cautiously as Yoon, which kept both his wins and losses small.

Soraya took Jess’s seat, and she paused by Pascal’s chair to lean down and kiss him. He patted her ass.

“Get some beauty sleep. Not that you need it.”

“Aw, sugar. You get another kiss for that.”

“Get a room,” Breukel said good-naturedly.

“We’ve got one! But Pascal’s having too much fun with you boys to come with me!” She affected a pout, then walked away, deliberately putting some extra swish in her hips and checking over her shoulder to make sure Pascal was watching.

They were all watching, which she’d expected. She kept walking, laughing softly.

Ten minutes later, she was creeping back down the darkened passageway she’d explored the night before dressed in her black sneaking-around outfit, listening to the laughter coming from the dining room not far away. From the talk she could overhear, she suspected they’d switched to poker, which would definitely keep them all busy and distracted for a while, and likely have the guards intently watching too. Pascal must have nudged them into switching games, to make sure everyone’s attention was well and truly caught.

The kitchen was quiet and dark, the staff all long since cleaned up and gone to their beds. She slipped past, a shadow in the dark, and found another door a little further along the alley. Tested it.

“Damn.” Well, she’d come prepared. Josef hadn’t looked too closely at her manicure kit, fortunately, or he’d have found the tools in it looked a little different to those found in any manicure kit one might buy in a store.

“Thank you, big sis,” she murmured as the lock clicked after just a few seconds of careful probing. Liane had spent hours coaching Jess with the lock-picking tools, saying she never knew when the skill might come in handy.

She opened the door the tiniest crack and waited; the room on the other side was dark, and after a few moments of silence she edged the door open a little more, just enough to slide her body through.

An archway on the other side of the room she’d entered led into another lounge area, one she hadn’t seen yet. It was set up as a surveillance station, half a dozen monitors set up on several desks laid out in a U shape, two guys sitting in the center. With their backs to her, leaning intently in towards one of the monitors, showing the poker game… and the camera focused in on Soraya's spectacular chest.

Jess grinned to herself, eyeing the door off to her left, the door which had to lead to the server room, considering the location of the window outside in the alley. It had a door handle with a lock similar to the one she'd just encountered, but she hoped it wasn't locked. The surveillance room was pretty dark, the only light coming from the monitors, but it was also quiet, and any sound she made might make the two watching guards turn around.

She eyed the large couch between her and the guards, crouched down and crept behind it towards the server room door. Reached out gingerly to lay her fingers on the handle and very slowly, very gently, tried to turn it.

"Shit," she mouthed, before getting her lockpicks out again.

One of the guards said something coarse in Spanish and they both laughed loudly, which at least gave Jess the opportunity to slide a pick into the lock and hurriedly twist.

It didn't give, and she breathed a silent curse, waiting for another opportunity. *Slow and steady wins the race*. Liane's instructions ran through her head.

Yeah, but I bet she never had to pick a lock literally behind the backs of two drunk guards. There was a row of empty beer bottles on the tables in between the monitors. She still couldn't risk making a sound. She didn't want to have to kill them.

On the fourth round of coarse laughter, the lock clicked, and Jess let out a soundless, relieved breath. She waited for another round of laughter before slipping quickly through the door and closing it silently behind her.

"Now this is what I'm talking about," she whispered, looking around. It wasn't up to her standards, of course, but the computers were modern, and she could see a row of green lights on the satellite modem. "Come to mama."

Dipping her fingers inside her top and down between her breasts, Jess pulled one more gadget from her bag of tricks. The most risky one of all - a USB stick. It had come to the island screwed inside the metal heels of a pair of her designer shoes, and she had hoped desperately it would pass Josef's tests, even though she'd built and designed it herself to be invisible to any scans looking for electronics.

She could have done this without the hacking worms stored on that key. But it was so, so much faster with it, which reduced the amount of time she'd have to spend in here.

The server was password protected, but she was inside in under sixty seconds, and three minutes later, Isla Fortuna Continental was silently, invisibly uploading every scrap of data it possessed to Hestia Global Security. And it would keep *on* uploading every new piece of data entered, until Jess told it to stop.

She took thirty more seconds to type a very fast message to Liane, listing the names of the buyers and what Pascal had told her about the officially-dead CIA agent Sebastian Maroney reinventing himself as Baz Fortuna. Jess could just imagine the shockwaves *that* was going to set off inside the Agency; even the unflappable Deputy Director Spires was likely to lose her cool over that piece of information.

Just under five minutes after entering the server room, Jess put the USB stick back into her bra and crept back to the door. She put her ear to it and waited, and after a couple of minutes snarled silently. The damn door was too soundproof. She couldn't hear a thing outside. She was just going to have to ease it open the tiniest crack and look through.

Nausea curled in the pit of her stomach, and she glanced for a moment at the window, debating exiting that way, but she wouldn't be able to close it behind her, and that risked whoever was managing this room figuring out someone had been in here. Jess was confident they'd never figure out what she'd done - she was too good to leave any trace they could follow - but she still didn't want them put on alert.

No, she had to risk the door. And remember to lock it behind her, as well as the outside door she'd come in.

Taking a deep breath, she turned the handle infinitesimally slowly, opened the door just enough to peek through.

And met the startled gaze of Mariska, who'd just entered the room from another door on the other side.

Jess froze in panic. For a couple of seconds, she and Mariska just stared at each other, and then one of the guards at the surveillance desk stood up.

"What are you doing in here, woman?" he asked in heavily accented English.

"General Dzhokharov, he send me to get more vodka. The bar in the other room, none left there. Mr Fortuna say, more bottles in here. Over here?" Mariska pointed at another bar.

"Yes, there'll be some there." The guard relaxed, sat back down. "Take what you want."

"Thank you." Mariska didn't glance Jess's way again, just went to the bar and began loudly clattering bottles around.

Which gave Jess the perfect cover she needed to slip quietly out of the server room and close the door, locking it behind her, and dive down behind the couch again. She waited there until Mariska had left, concerned she might be spotted sneaking through the archway if the guards turned their heads to watch Mariska going out the other door.

“Pretty girl,” one of the guards commented, the Spanish remark simple enough for Jess to follow.

“Too young,” the other guard grunted. “No breasts on her. The blond American, though? That’s what I call a woman.”

Jess cringed, crawling silently out through the archway into the darkened outer room. She didn’t want to hear what else they might say about her. Really didn’t want to think about what they’d do if they caught her.

Would Mariska say anything? Had she recognized Jess, through the small gap in the door? About all she’d have been able to see was one eye and a bit of Jess’s face, in shadow too, but Jess had paler skin than any other woman on the island except Mariska herself.

It wouldn't take much deduction to put two and two together.

There was absolutely nothing she could do about it even if Mariska had gone straight back to the dining room and told Fortuna she'd seen Jess sneaking around where she shouldn't be. All Jess could do was run as quickly and quietly as she could back to the villa, get into bed and make out that she'd been there all along if the guards came storming in to grab her.

She lay in bed, shaking with adrenaline and terror, for over an hour before finally concluding that Mariska hadn't said anything. Sleep eluded her still, though, and she was still awake staring at the darkened ceiling when Pascal came in around three in the morning.

"Hey," she said quietly as he slipped into bed beside her. Having seen the surveillance room, she was pretty confident now that nobody was listening to them in real time at least, though there could well be recordings.

"Sorry to wake you," he murmured.

"Haven't been asleep." She thought her next words over carefully. "Saw Mariska on my travels earlier. She didn't mention it?"

Pascal stiffened beside her. "No," he said. "Didn't hear her say more than a word or two all evening. I think she's trying to stay off the general's radar, poor little scrap. He's having fun with Fortuna's women, just telling Mariska to fetch and carry for him. She's probably grateful. It's kind of you to take notice of her."

Jess hoped he was right, that her kindness to Mariska meant the Chechen girl wouldn't say anything. Pascal touched her arm lightly and she rolled onto her side and cuddled against him, still feeling a bone-deep chill from the terror which had gripped her earlier.

"You're all right," he murmured softly, stroking his big hands down her back in a soothing rhythm. "You're doing great, Jess. So good. Everything okay?"

"Everything's great," she whispered. "Couldn't be better."

"Yeah?"

"Yeah." She nodded against his shoulder. "Perfection."

"Good." He kissed her forehead. "Now get some sleep. Business starts tomorrow."

Chapter 14

It was just after dawn when an noise woke Pascal from a deep sleep; something that didn't fit with the quiet chirping of the cicadas and the sound of waves lapping at the beach. Jess was sleeping peacefully in his arms, her long golden hair spread over the pillow like a silken fan, and he spent several moments just looking at her, unable to help himself. He'd met a lot of beautiful women over the years since he'd joined the Agency, some of them clever, sharp and calculating, but he didn't think he'd ever met one with the astounding combination of beauty, brains and compassion Jess possessed.

"No wonder Fortuna's got eyes for you, angel," he whispered, kissing her brow lightly.

“Even not showing him who you truly are, it’s obvious you’re out of my league.”

The noise that had woken him sounded again, and he lifted his head, eyes narrowing. That was a boat engine, and not a fancy motor yacht like the one that had picked them up in Puerto Rico. It sounded more like a tramp steamer, a small freighter.

Slipping out of bed, he headed for the window on silent feet, twitched the drapes aside slightly. The villas had been built facing the beach, but he could just see at the edge of the view, the island’s single jetty. And the four men standing on it with a large flatbed trolley.

A boat nosed into view then, a rustbucket of a thing, the kind of tiny anonymous tramp freighter which wouldn’t raise a second glance pulling up to any pier in the Caribbean to deliver a few supplies.

Pascal was only interested because of Fortuna’s statement about waiting for pieces to be in place. The arms dealer had been notably irritated about having to wait another day to start his business.

The men on the dock caught ropes thrown from the little freighter and tied it off, but the engines never shut off running. A hatch was opened, a ramp pushed across level with the pier, and the trolley pushed onto the boat.

A minute later it came back off with a large wooden crate strapped atop it, wheeled off along the dock out of sight.

Pascal would have loved to see where they were taking it, but he didn't dare open the French doors in case someone was keeping an eye out for watchers. If he was correct, Fortuna would be showing off later anyway.

The ramp was pulled back onto the boat, the lines untied, and the tramp freighter chugged away again, a stream of black smoke hanging in the clear early morning air for a few minutes before dissipating.

"Hm." Was that crate big enough for the three suitcase nukes? He didn't think so. Nor did he think Fortuna would put all his eggs in one basket; the man would never trust anyone that far. No, he thought only one of the weapons had been brought in on that freighter, and the other two were probably far from here, widely separated and closely guarded, awaiting instructions for delivery. The images shown on the introductory film of the three weapons in the same place could have been taken months ago.

That's how Pascal would have done it. And however much it sickened him to think about, he and Fortuna had been through the same Agency training. He wished he knew more about Sebastian Maroney; what had Fortuna's path to the Agency been? What was his background? His specialties? What had he been assigned to while he worked for the Agency?

Not knowing made him nervous. He'd never gone into a situation without having been able to do a complete workup on the people he was going to meet, but Fortuna was a blank slate; the little Pascal had dug up on his background while researching him was obviously fake, now he knew that Baz Fortuna was really Sebastian Maroney. Pascal knew more about Yoon, despite the North Korean government's habits of extreme secrecy, than he knew about Fortuna, and he didn't like that he had no way to get more information.

Jess had told him what she planned to do with the server if she got access, and he absolutely approved because it minimized their potential exposure, but it also left them with no way to receive communication from their allies on the outside. Even a simple Google search was impossible, not that he would have risked putting Sebastian Maroney's name into the search engine anyway. Fortuna would surely have a track-and-trace set up for anyone foolish enough to do such a thing.

With a sigh, Pascal returned to the bed. There was nothing more to see down at the dock, and he hadn't had enough sleep yet. He needed his wits about him if the bidding was to start today.

Jess snuggled up to him, murmured sleepily "What's up?"

"Looks like a special delivery just came in."

He felt her stiffen, and her eyes popped open. "Yeah?"

"Yeah. Probably just more food or vodka for Dzhokharov or something." He chuckled, but he was shaking his head as he looked into Jess's eyes. "Just one crate."

"Hm." She made her voice sound sleepy, but he could see her mind was racing. "Can't be anything big, then."

"Go back to sleep. Nothing for us to do anyway."

She was still tense, though. He smoothed his hand down her spine again, in the long, soothing strokes he'd used the night before, felt Jess react almost immediately, her body curving softly against his.

His body reacted predictably.

"Sorry," he breathed against her brow.

"I'm not." She tipped her head back and pressed her mouth against his.

"Jess," he mumbled against her lips, "why..."

"Please." Her fingers curled around his and she pulled his hand against her breast. "I want this, Pascal. I need - I need to take my mind off things. Do you want...?"

"Oh hell yes." Whatever her reasons, he did want. Very much.

She did too; there was no faking the eagerness with which she clutched at him, almost dragged his shorts off and curled her fingers around his cock, already standing at salute for her. All the while she met his kisses with enthusiasm, gasping into his mouth, moaning when his caressing fingers brushed aside her silky pajamas and found tight, beaded nipples.

A long leg hooked over his hip, and Jess ground against him, making him see stars as the silky fabric of her pajama pants slid over aching, sensitive flesh.

Condoms. He had some in his travel kit in the bathroom; scrambled out of bed and bolted to fetch them, leaving Jess squawking with displeasure, though she laughed when she saw him coming back with the package in his hand.

“Good thinking.”

“Somebody has to. I’m not sure this is one of your more brilliant ideas, but hell.” He shrugged. “I’d be mad to turn you down.”

Easing back into bed beside Jess, he paused a moment, just to gaze at her and take in how gorgeous she was, lying there with her breasts exposed and her golden hair spread around her. Reaching out, he coiled a lock around his finger.

"This is lovely. But you know... I think I liked it better blue."

"You did?" Her eyes brightened. "I'm going to color it back again when we get home."

"It suits you that way. As unique as you are. This is more... conventionally pretty. I thought it suited the situation."

"It does." She'd be even more eye-catching with her blue mermaid hair, but she also would not have fit with the image of the kind of woman expected to be on Pascal Montalban's arm.

She was very much the kind of woman Pascal *Montoya* wanted on his arm, though. Blonde hair or blue.

He tried to push the intrusive thoughts away. He and Jess weren't a real couple, and when this mission ended, it was very probable they wouldn't see each other again.

Unless he accepted her job offer, which was a whole different thing he couldn't allow himself to think about right now.

Right now was all about the lovely woman in his arms, and his extremely pressing need to make love to her.

Jess ran her hands down Pascal's shoulders and biceps, squeezing lightly, testing the thick muscles. "You sure haven't let yourself go, have you?" she murmured.

"Hit the gym at least four times a week," Pascal said, "at least, when I'm not stuck on a private island which doesn't appear to have one. Nor enough space to go running."

"I wonder how Fortuna stays in shape? Or maybe he's got a private gym in that villa of his at the top of the island. It's big enough."

"Can we not talk about him right now?" Pascal begged, and Jess laughed.

"My mind goes on tangents. I'm sorry."

"Let's see if I can keep you focused." He slid down the bed, checking with a glance whether she was okay with it. She nodded, running her fingers into his hair as he lowered his head to her breast, licked delicately at her nipple, working it up to a tight, aching bud before closing his lips over it and suckling.

Jess moaned, her back arching, fingers tightening in his hair, legs coming up to tangle with his own. Pascal let out a moan of his own, but kept to his self-appointed task, determined not to be selfish and seek his own pleasure without ensuring Jessikah's first.

She let him know what she liked, what she wanted, because of course she did. Passivity wasn't in her nature. She urged him over to the other breast, and after a few minutes put her hand on top of his head and gave him a gentle push downwards.

He was more than happy to take her direction, sliding further down the bed to lie between her thighs and nuzzle into her pussy, tasting her lightly at first, tracing the tip of his finger around her clit, finding her already wet. Her hips rolled, beckoning him on, so he curled his arms beneath her thighs, and buried his face in her.

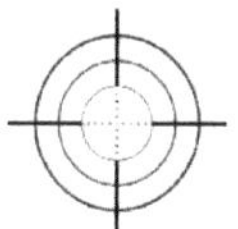

Pascal knew exactly what he was doing, and it took only a few seconds of his talented tongue and fingers working her over before Jess's eyes rolled back in her head and she clutched at the sheet beneath her, body bowing up as she cried out wordlessly.

He didn't stop, keeping up the pressure at a perfect pitch to sustain the orgasm as long as possible, until she became just too sensitive and begged him to stop in a high, breathy voice, squirming her hips down and away from him.

"Need a break?" He kissed the inside of her thigh, working down towards her knee. "I'll give you five minutes, and then I'm putting this condom on and fucking you until you scream my name."

"I think I might already have screamed your name," she mumbled, boneless, drunken with pleasure, but already feeling her body starting to stir with interest at his promise.

"I want to hear you scream it louder."

The low, sexy rumble of his voice against her skin made her tremble as need raced through her again.

"I don't want you to wait five minutes." She whimpered it, grabbing at his shoulders, trying to pull him up over her.

"Impatient woman." He laughed quietly, fumbling for the condom packet. "If you're sure?"

Their eyes met, and she nodded. "I'm sure."

She wasn't sure what would happen afterwards - if things would be awkward between them - but right now, there was nothing in the world she wanted more than to make love with Pascal. She shied away from the mental choice of words, but she knew - this was more than just sex. More than just scratching an itch, more even than just inevitable sexual tension coming to the boil because of the proximity and the stress they were under.

His hands were gentle as he eased her thighs further apart and knelt between them. She thought it was wonder in his eyes as he gazed down at her, and she suspected there was probably awe in hers, because he was a magnificent sight, all powerful muscle rippling under brown skin as he reached down to her.

"Jessikah." He breathed her name against her lips as he lowered his head to kiss her. "You are. *Incredible*."

"Oh, my... ohhhh." Her breath whooshed out in a gasp as he eased the tip of his cock into her, pressing gently. "Woooow. Oh."

"Okay?" he checked once again.

"More than okay, don't you dare stop now!" She dug her nails into his shoulders, tried to pull him deeper.

"Don't be in such a hurry," he chided her, but she could hear the strain in his voice, see the fine tremor in his biceps as he held himself over her.

"Come on, come with me!" She hooked her legs around his hips, lifted herself off the bed and dragged him to the hilt in one movement.

Pascal let out a noise that was very nearly a roar, his fists clenching in the pillow on either side of Jess's head. For a moment he held still, deep inside her, his gold eyes dark as he gazed into hers. And then he brought one hand down to curve under her ass, tilting her hips to precisely where he wanted them, and *thrust*.

It was exactly, precisely what Jess wanted. The friction, the pressure, and the pleasure built up rapidly until she was indeed screaming his name, clinging to him desperately, begging for another release.

“Take it,” Pascal gritted out, and suddenly he was flipping them over, rolling to his back and pushing her up to sit astride him. “Ride me and take what you want.” His thumb pushed between them, finding her clit and rubbing circles over the wet, slippery nub. “I want to feel you come on me.”

He was going to get that wish, and damn soon. Jess’s hips rolled, her thighs flexed and she rode him at a feverish gallop, chasing her second orgasm at a frantic pace.

“That’s it. Oh, fuck, that feels so good!” Pascal’s voice was a harsh shout as Jess slid over the edge and her inner walls fluttered and clenched on his cock. “Ahhh... *Jess*!” He shouted her name, hands clenching hard on her hips to hold her close as he bowed up against her, his eyes fixed on her face. Watching her with a fierce intensity.

“Omigod, Pascal.” She collapsed on his chest, breathing fast, hearing his heartbeat thundering under her ear, though it rapidly settled back to a slow, steady thump. They were both sweating, sticking to each other, but right then she didn’t care. She just wanted to cuddle, in the euphoric afterglow of two spectacular orgasms, and feel the pleasurable hum throughout her whole body.

“Indeed.” His warm hand stroked up and down her spine in that slow, soothing gesture he liked to employ; she was getting alarmingly used to it, Jess recognized, starting to really enjoy being touched like that by Pascal.

She was drifting off to sleep right there, tired and thoroughly pleasured, when she felt Pascal shift beneath her.

“Gotta get rid of the condom,” he murmured against her hair, before easing her off him and down to the mattress. She felt a kiss pressed to her cheek, and him move off the bed... but by the time he returned, she was sound asleep.

Chapter 15

Curling back up with Jess in his arms, warm, sated and naked, was one of the most quietly enjoyable moments of Pascal's life. He couldn't ever remember feeling quite so content.

It was a dangerous feeling. Especially considering what he'd seen down at the dock not an hour earlier, and what he thought might be going to happen later today, because Fortuna wasn't going to wait long before starting off the auctions.

He needed to rest while he could, but despite the pleasure humming through his veins, he lay wakeful, listening to Jess's soft breathing until there was a knock on the outer door of the villa, and Josef's voice calling his name.

Pascal eased out of bed carefully, not wanting to wake Jess, and yanked his shorts on before going to the door.

“Keep it down,” he said as he opened the door in the middle of Josef knocking again. “Jess is still sleeping and she’s grumpy if she gets woken before she’s ready.”

Josef just looked at him. “Mr Fortuna requests your presence in the dining hall,” was all he said.

“Now?”

“In thirty minutes.”

Pascal considered the other man. Josef was nothing more than an aide, that was obvious, but still... there was useful information to be had here, if Pascal just asked the right questions. “Finally getting down to business, are we?” he asked, leaning casually against the doorframe. “About time. Nice place and all, but I’m not really in a holiday mood.”

“Just information, for now,” Josef said. “And Mr Montalban? Leave your woman to sleep.”

Pascal narrowed his eyes. “Bet Yoon hasn’t been told that,” he said argumentatively.

"Mr Yoon's translator is required." Josef gave him a long-suffering look. "Your woman's smart mouth isn't."

That was an opinion Josef wouldn't have dared voice without being very sure his employer shared it, which meant Fortuna had privately been expressing disapproval of Jess's opinionated attitude. Which was actually slightly reassuring; Pascal didn't think Fortuna was likely to continue making moves on Jess now that he'd realized she wasn't a pretty, simpering ornament.

Of course, it didn't mean Jess wasn't still in danger. Fortuna was hardly the only man on the island who found her attractive, and every single one of them was an amoral bastard who'd absolutely rape her if he thought he could get away with it. Pascal hoped they were all too wary of him to dare, but nothing was a given when you were dealing with men who lived far outside the law - or recognized no legal authority anyway.

"I'll be there," he said, and shut the door in Josef's face.

"Who was that?" Jess was sitting up in bed, her hair tumbling around her, and he paused for a brief moment to admire how sexy she looked all sleep-mussed, the white sheet barely covering her breasts.

"Josef. Looks like things might finally be kicking off. I've got to go meet Fortuna in the dining room."

"Oh?"

She was clearly boiling with questions she couldn't ask. He grinned at her as he headed for the bathroom, but kept his voice flat and level.

"I'm afraid you're not invited. This is the business part of the trip, Jess. *My* business. You go lay by the pool with the other girls. Or stay here and I'll send someone with something to eat, if you're hungry."

"If you're meeting in the dining room, I suppose there'll be some food by the pool. I *am* hungry," she said, as though thinking aloud.

He got it. Sitting in the villa by herself waiting for him to come back would be torture for her, as it would for him if their situations were reversed.

“You go. Enjoy yourself. You made some friends yesterday, hm?”

“Sugar.” She injected scorn into her tone, though her expression definitely didn’t match what she was saying, and he knew she was acting up for unseen ears. “You expect me to make friends with those girls? They’re sex workers. Except for Mariska, who’s literally an underage trafficking victim. I feel sorry for her - for all of them, frankly - but I don’t think we’re ever going to be *friends*.”

“Don’t be catty. Doesn’t suit you.” He winked at her, to show her he knew it wasn’t her true feelings she was expressing.

“You haven’t seen me in my leather Catwoman outfit. I’m *fabulous*.” She grinned back at him.

“I... can imagine all too well, actually!” He needed to get in the shower and out of the villa before he got distracted again. He shut the bathroom door and turned the shower on, firmly quashing the impulse to ask Jess to come in and share the hot water.

"So good of you to join us," Fortuna said a bit sarcastically as Pascal entered the dining room.

Pascal looked around with raised brows. "Am I late? I don't see Mr Hayworth. Is he not coming?"

"I'm here," the evangelist snapped, striding into the room behind Pascal, though he stopped short of pushing Pascal out of the way. "What's so all-fired important that you had to rush out out of bed? I was *busy*."

"I hope you haven't been taking that bad mood out on any more of my girls, Mr Hayworth." Fortuna gave him a look of unconcealed dislike. "I don't care to see them bruised."

"They're just hookers." Hayworth shrugged. "Pay her more."

"You do know that prostitutes who allow you to hit them usually state it up front and charge accordingly?" Pascal said, disgusted.

"*You* don't get to decide whether it's on the menu or not."

Hayworth glared at him.

Entirely unafraid, Pascal glared back. "Just got to show how big a man you are by beating up on women, don't you?" he said scornfully.

"Easy, Montalban." Dzokharov put a hand on his arm, but carefully, approaching from the side. "We don't need to fight among ourselves."

"He's not one of us, and I don't like him being here." Pascal determinedly brought up the issue he'd raised with Fortuna and Breukel at breakfast yesterday. He'd spent a long time building his character's reputation; to Pascal Montalban, trust was everything. He preferred to do business directly, with people who had proven track records of honest dealing, and it was entirely within character for him to get antagonistic with someone like Saul Hayworth, a total outsider to the arms dealing world and a rude one at that.

"Well, there is an option for you to leave today," Fortuna said cheerfully.

"I thought we were here for the duration of the sale?" Pascal turned on him like a wolf. "So that there was no risk of anyone leaving and betraying what's going on here?"

"Easy." Fortuna made a pacifying gesture. "You've all been very patient," he told his waiting audience, "and the pieces are all now in place, so it's time for me to make clear the terms of the auctions. If you'll all come with me?"

They trailed after him, back out into the lobby, through a door behind what used to be the reception desk, and into a large office area, completely vacant apart from two men standing either side of a heavy door. They were the first visibly armed guards Pascal had seen on the island; though he was pretty sure Fortuna was carrying, and likely Josef and his other aides as well, they had their weapons concealed. These guards, on the other hand, were holding AR-15s.

Fortuna pulled a key on a chain from around his neck, and used it to unlock the door, opening it to show what had presumably once been the hotel's security vault.

Now, the only thing in it was the crate Pascal had seen being delivered off the little tramp freighter earlier, the lid levered off to show its contents.

One of the hard-shelled suitcases containing the nukes.

“Only one?” the translator said, after Mr Yoon spoke rapidly in Korean. “Where are the other two?”

“Quite safe, I assure you. Precautionary measures, you understand; I needed leverage just in case one of you was in fact a plant and we all got swept up by the US government.” Fortuna smiled proudly at the nuke. “I would have traded them for my freedom.”

“And left us all to rot,” Breukel muttered, with a sideways glance at Pascal and a wry twist of his mouth.

“Just business, my friend. Just business.” Fortuna gestured expansively towards the suitcase. “So. If anyone would like to inspect the merchandise? I have a Geiger counter here, and I understand Dr Choe has a doctorate in nuclear physics.”

Pascal felt his eyes widen with astonishment, and he wasn't the only one who turned to give the tiny North Korean translator a hard stare.

"*She's* the buyer?" Hayworth said in disbelief.

"No, Mr Yoon is the buyer. You were each offered the opportunity to bring a companion, you'll recall. I did not specify what qualifications might or might not exclude them." Fortuna smirked, and it was definitely directed at Hayworth. "If you underestimated Dr Choe because of her gender, that's entirely on you."

"I'm good with taking her word on it," Breukel said, and Pascal nodded in agreement.

"Me too. If the device isn't good, I'm assuming you'll be advising Mr Yoon not to bid?" He addressed the diminutive translator directly, and she nodded.

"Correct, Mr Montalban."

"But I for one would like to observe closely, if you don't mind," Pascal added.

"As you please."

“You do what you like. I’m staying out here. I’ve been to Chernobyl,” Dzokharov grunted. “Don’t need any more radiation in my bones.”

Hayworth hesitated too, and remained outside the room with the Chechen, Yoon, and Fortuna’s men. Fortuna himself entered with Pascal, Breukel and Dr Choe.

“The combination?” Dr Choe requested, and Fortuna fished a card from his pocket and handed it over.

Pascal watched as Dr Choe opened the case and began inspecting the device inside. She seemed to be working to some mental checklist, methodically working her way around the complicated array of delicate electronics.

Pascal knew enough to be pretty confident he was looking at a genuine suitcase nuke. There were a few pieces missing - a detonator, for one, there seemed to be no way to set it off, a fact which was definitely reassuring at the moment.

"The detonator?” Choe asked then, confirming Pascal’s deduction.

"Not supplied. Don't want any accidental detonations, do we? I'm sure someone with your expertise would have no difficulty putting your own together, but if required, I can supply them. For a small additional cost, of course."

"Of course," Pascal echoed dryly.

Dr Choe finished her inspection and stepped back with a nod. "An impressive piece of engineering." There was an avid light in her eyes, and Pascal could tell she was dying to disassemble the device further, figure out every little piece that made it work. Figure out how to duplicate it.

And that was something he absolutely could not allow.

Yoon called something from outside the room, and Choe answered in her own language, before speaking again in English. "Yes. The device is good. I recommend purchase."

"Thank you." Pascal inclined his head to her politely, and with one last lingering look at the device, Choe left the room to speak further with her boss.

“So when do we start the auction?” Breukel asked as Fortuna closed the case up again.

“This afternoon. The first auction, that is.” Fortuna gestured for them to precede him out of the vault, closing the door behind them and relocking it. Turning to look at the group of buyers, he said, “And this is where I tell you the rest of the conditions of this sale.”

They all looked at him in silence, waiting. Fortuna was clearly enjoying himself, grandstanding a little in front of his armed guards, strutting up and down and smirking.

“I will conduct three auctions. At each, you will each be given an electronic pad and offered the opportunity to make a bid. Once all bids are in, you will get a number, from 1 to 5, telling you where you are ranked in the bidding. You’ll get two more opportunities to bid. The person ranked first at the end of the auction will be declared the winner and, once the funds transfer has been completed, will leave the island immediately. Your purchase will be delivered to the location you specify anywhere on the globe within 72 hours.”

"Wait." It was Breukel who spoke. "Are you saying that the winner of the first auction has to leave immediately after? Not stay for the second and third?"

"That's correct."

"But my client wishes to purchase all three devices!"

Fortuna smiled his shark smile, his eyes watchful. "I don't think it would be fair to allow one buyer to hog all the devices. There are five of you. Only three devices. This way, only two of you miss out... and I'd rather have only two of you pissed off at me than four."

"You should have revealed this to us before we came," Breukel said angrily.

"Is it an all or nothing proposition for your client, then? In the pitch video, I clearly said you would have three opportunities to bid for *one* of the devices. It's not my problem if your client made assumptions. Are you withdrawing from the sale entirely? I do have a backup buyer who would like to come in if anyone drops out, but I'd have to delay the first auction until they got here... and of course, for reasons already noted, you wouldn't be able to leave until all three auctions are concluded, Mr Breukel."

Breukel looked annoyed, but eventually shrugged. "I was given a brief to buy all three of the weapons if possible, but I'm sure my client will agree that one is better than none. No, I'm still in."

"Excellent. Everyone else still in?" Fortuna checked with each of them, and one by one, they nodded their agreement. "Then we'll begin this afternoon. Lunch is ready now; we'll reconvene at two and begin the first auction."

"When will the second and third take place?" Pascal asked, when the others began drifting towards the door.

"Every 48 hours, I think. Gives me time to make all the arrangements for delivery after each one. You can enjoy my hospitality in the meantime… and reconsider your budgets, perhaps, if you're not close to the winning bid. Not that I'll be revealing what the winning bids are, of course." He smirked.

“I’d like to consult with my client,” Breukel said as they all returned to the dining room, where a large buffet was being set out.

“No,” was Fortuna’s only response. “I made it clear that there would be no communication with the outside world until the sales were concluded, with the exception of arranging payment transfers once the price has been agreed. I cannot make exceptions, Dieter. You understand. I’m afraid you’ll just have to use your professional judgment.”

Breukel looked extremely annoyed, and Pascal knew exactly how he felt. Spreading the auctions out like this threw a huge wrench in the gears. He had to make sure he didn’t accidentally bid too high and buy either of the first two weapons, because he needed to know who bought them all. But he also had to trust that Jess’s worm in the computers was doing its job and would catch and retransmit enough information to enable the CIA to be in a position to intercept the first two before they were delivered to the buyers. Because otherwise, they weren’t going to get off the island to pass on what information they had to the Agency in time before the first device at least was delivered.

Jess came waltzing in then with the other girls trailing along behind her, obviously summoned by one of Fortuna's lackeys to come to lunch.

"Hi, darling, I'm starving, there was nothing to eat by the pool." She bounced up and gave him a kiss. "Get your business done?"

"The first part of it. Serious business starts this afternoon, and we might be out of here by tonight."

"Oh?" she raised her eyebrows at him.

"First of three auctions takes place today. Winner leaves right after."

"Oh." She blinked. "I thought you wanted to buy all three?"

"Yes, apparently, I wasn't the only one with those plans. Breukel wants all three as well, but Fortuna has set the rules. No more than one per buyer."

They were speaking quietly, but not making any effort to conceal that they were talking business. Nobody gave them so much as a second glance, everyone intent on getting something to eat and sitting down.

"When will the other auctions be?" Jess asked, serving some salad onto her plate.

"Every second day." Pascal glanced across at the North Korean pair, talking in their own language on the other side of the table. "Turns out, Yoon's translator isn't just a translator. She's a nuclear physicist. *Doctor* Choe."

"Wow. They kept that quiet." Jess shook her head. "Not that she's opened her mouth really, but to translate. She all but called Soraya a whore yesterday. Clearly doesn't want to mix with us girls."

"Came in useful, though. She was able to assess the merchandise, better than I might have been able to."

"And it's what you hoped?"

"It certainly appears to be. Just hope my client's budget is up to the task."

"I guess we're about to find out."

Chapter 16

Jess had fully expected to be sent out with the other girls when it was time for the auction to start, but Fortuna seemed to want a larger audience. Strutting up and down, he made a big show of distributing five tablets; Jess itched to get her hands on one but made herself sit still and content herself with peering at Pascal's screen. He was considerate enough to oh-so-casually hold it at an angle which was easy for her to see.

There appeared to be only one app installed, a basic custom thing which, when opened, offered nothing more than a numeric keypad, a Delete key and an Enter key.

“You have two minutes to enter you starting bid and press the Enter key,” Fortuna declared. “All bids are to be placed in US dollar amounts, though of course you will be offered the opportunity to settle up in any stable currency or cryptocurrency of your choice, should you be the high bidder. At the end of the two minutes, your rank in the auction will be displayed and you will have the opportunity to bid twice more.”

“Will we know what the highest bid is at?” Dzhokharov asked.

“Not unless the top bidder chooses to tell you.” Fortuna smirked. “Get typing, gentlemen. Your two minutes starts now.” He lifted his own tablet and made a great show of tapping on the screen.

Instantly, a timer appeared at the bottom of Pascal’s screen and began counting down.

Jess didn’t waste her time watching what Pascal was typing. He had his own strategy for this, she was sure, presumably dictated by CIA, though finding out that he had to deliberately lose the first two auctions was probably causing him some angst. He’d have to recalculate on the fly, working out how much was the right amount to bid to lose, but not by too much.

Instead, Jess watched the other bidders. Yoon and Doctor Choe had their heads bent together, Choe pointing out to her boss which numerals to type in order to place their bid. Breukel seemed agitated, typing and deleting, glancing around at the other buyers. Hayworth looked bored. He'd already entered his bid, obviously, and now sat looking at the girls who'd clustered by the bar. Dzhokharov was one-finger typing, painstakingly entering his bid, obviously making at least one or two errors as he clicked his tongue and poked at the screen again.

A quiet chime sounded from all the tablets in unison as the countdown timer reached zero, the screens went blank for a moment, then came back to life displaying a single large red digit.

Jess could only see Pascal's screen. And the number 4 on it.

Pascal pursed his lips, but said nothing. Jess looked away again, checking in on everyone else. Nobody looked pleased except Fortuna, who presumably could see all the bids on his tablet, and was failing to conceal a pleased smirk.

At least one of the bids was to his satisfaction, then. Jess tried to guess who, but everyone was wearing their best poker face.

Except Hayworth, who didn't have a poker face, and who still looked bored… but now with a side of smugness.

"Second round," Fortuna said. "Place your bids."

This time, Pascal's number changed to a 3. Hayworth looked even more smug, and Breukel, Jess thought, was cracking around the edges. He'd gone a little pale and was tight around the lips.

"If that's the best your client has, Dieter, I don't know how they expected to purchase all three devices," Fortuna said in a not-so-gentle swipe.

"This is an unprecedented situation, is it not? One can't exactly run an online search for *how much should you pay for a suitcase nuke*," Breukel snapped back.

"I mean, you *could*," Jess muttered. "You'd just have to be prepared for the NSA to be watching your every keystroke forever after."

She should know. She'd written some of the software that made sure nobody could even be searching on the Dark Web for that stuff without the NSA knowing about it.

Fortuna called for the last round of bidding to begin. Pascal entered his bid quickly, then joined Jess in looking around, assessing the room.

"I think Hayworth has this," Jess breathed very softly, for Pascal's ears alone. "I think he blew the rest of you out of the water from the beginning."

The chime sounded for the final time, and Hayworth jumped to his feet, pumping his fist in triumph. "Yes!"

"Congratulations, Mr Hayworth." Fortuna looked pleased with the result as he stepped forward to shake the evangelist's hand. "Looks like the rest of you will have to up your game, gentlemen," he noted. "If you'll step this way, Mr Hayworth? We'll go arrange the transfers, and you can be on your way."

The room was briefly silent, and then Dzokharov lurched to his feet, swearing in his own language. He headed for the door, but was intercepted by Josef.

"The tablet, please." Josef held his hand out.

Dzokharov hesitated for a moment, but then shoved the tablet at Josef and stormed out. About ten seconds later he strode back in. "Mariska!" he bellowed.

The Chechen girl jumped up from where she had been sitting in silence, almost running to Dzokharov, her face pale with fright.

"Shit," Jess muttered under her breath. Dzokharov was angry, he was going to take it out on Mariska, and there was absolutely nothing Jess or Pascal could do about it. She shared a concerned glance with Pascal.

Josef was coming around to collect the tablets; Jess allowed herself one brief, wistful glance as Pascal handed his over. The operating system looked to have been rooted but she was certain she could have managed to get something out of it. She just had to trust that the worm she'd installed was doing its job, and Fortuna would presumably be using the computers to issue instructions to transport one of the other devices to the location Hayworth specified. Not to mention whatever method Hayworth was using to transfer payment, which in and of itself would be an intriguing trail to follow.

"What was your final bid?" Jess asked in an undertone as she and Pascal ambled slowly back towards their villa.

"Sixteen point two million, and I ended third," he murmured quietly back.

"Here's something I don't understand. Why is Dzokharov here and bidding? I thought the Chechens had access to the Russian nuclear arsenal, and they had suitcase nukes?"

"Yes and no. The Chechens do have access. But the Russians never had anything which was one-man portable like these. You'd need an SUV to move the ones they have. This one is literally in a wheeled suitcase."

"Where did Fortuna get them from, then?" Jess couldn't understand that. "Are they American?"

"No." Pascal hesitated for a moment. "I'm fairly sure they're Israeli."

He knew more, but he couldn't tell her right now, it was obvious. Jess could make a fair guess; Pascal had mentioned back at her office in Anaheim that he'd been on the trail of these devices for a while, so the Israelis had likely asked the US for help when they realized they'd lost track of three of their weapons. But she also recalled that both Pascal and his boss DDO Spires had seemed startled when Fortuna revealed he had three of the devices, not one, so very possibly the Israelis hadn't been entirely honest about the magnitude of their problem.

Which also didn't surprise Jess, but it did concern her, because what if there were more than these three devices out there on the black market? What if Fortuna wasn't the only one who'd got his hands on them?

She could hardly wait to get out of here, so she could get back to her computers and go deep diving into the Dark Web, trying to track down the answers to those questions.

Right now, though, she had to keep playing her role, especially as they were just entering their villa and likely coming back into range of audio surveillance again.

“I wonder what Hayworth paid,” she mused aloud. “And if and where he’s planning to set it off!”

“I’d never heard of him before, but you obviously know who he is. Tell me about him,” Pascal invited, laying down on the bed and pulling her to lie beside him.

This was a perfectly legitimate conversation for them to be having; Jess had to think about her answers, though, because she did know a few things about the Hayworths which might not be public knowledge, including the fact that old man Hayworth had been a Ku Klux Klan member before going mainstream and founding his church. The Hayworths were very careful to keep that on the down low, though.

"Well," she started cautiously, "his daddy's the real star. He started his own church down in … I think Tennessee, but it might have been the Carolinas somewhere, back in the early nineties. Built a huge following. He's one of those preachers you hear about who tells his congregation that he needs a private jet so he can deliver God's Word to those godless heathens in Las Vegas, and they buy it for him."

"And Hayworth senior is still in charge of the church?"

"Oh yeah. He's branded himself as some sort of modern-day prophet. I've seen clips of him preaching and he's one hell of a speaker, charisma to burn. But it's all sin and brimstone, you know the type."

"Not so much," Pascal said, "evangelism isn't really so big in Europe. It seems to be a peculiarly American thing, at least the Christian variety of it is. The mindset is just as alien to me as Muslim extremism."

"Me too, to be honest!" Jess chewed on her lower lip. "I'm seriously concerned, Pascal. Are the Hayworths really going to use that weapon? I've heard some of the things Joshua Hayworth says about the government. What if he decides to set off a nuke outside Congress or something?"

There was open dread in both their expressions as they gazed at each other, but Pascal's voice came out calmly disinterested. "War and turmoil are good for business, angel. It's not like either of us live in DC. You spend most of your time in Europe with me now anyway."

"You're so unfeeling!" She pouted at him. "What about Mom and Dad?"

"They don't live in DC either. And your dad's rich enough that even if America does go to shit, he can get them out of it."

His expression was apologetic; she nodded to show she understood he was just playing the necessary role. That he was truly as concerned about what Hayworth might be planning as she was.

They just had to hope Jess's worm was passing on the necessary information and that Hestia and the CIA together would be able to act on it and intercept the weapon before delivery, because it was likely Pascal and Jess would still be stuck on Isla Fortuna incommunicado by that time.

"*Hayworth*?" Deputy Director Spires stared at her computer screen and the image of Liane Hagerty, looking back at her. "As in *Joshua* Hayworth? The televangelist?"

"His son Saul, it appears. We took a look once the information arrived that Saul was at the auction, and the church accounts for the last few months make for very interesting reading. Lots of money being invested in cryptocurrencies, and the blockchain ledgers have suddenly started showing large transactions from the church's wallets to wallets controlled by an unknown party - Fortuna, we presume."

"So Hayworth won the auction," Spires muttered. "How much?"

"Best guess, from the transactions we're seeing? A hundred million."

"Holy Mother of God."

"I don't think there's much holy about what the Hayworths might be planning," Liane said bleakly.

"What else do you have for me?"

"A location. It's a ranch in West Virginia; owned by a shell corporation which we haven't traced back to the Hayworths or the church yet, but I wouldn't bet against it. Fortuna sent out instructions for one of the devices to be delivered there."

"*One* of the devices?" Arrested, Spires stilled. "Hayworth didn't buy all three?"

"If he did, the instructions appear to be only to deliver one to the ranch."

"Well." Spires tapped a manicured nail on her lower lip. "If he paid that much for *one*. Goodness me."

"What does the satellite data show?" Liane asked then. As soon as the data had started arriving from Jess's worm the previous evening, Hestia's techs had pinpointed the island and Liane had passed the information on to Spires immediately. Spires had muttered something about re-tasking a satellite, and Liane had to assume she'd done it.

"A helicopter took off from the island around two hours ago, headed for Caracas. I daresay you might find the Hayworth private jet just happens to be there." Spires shook her head. "Honestly, I'm truly stunned by this. I know who the Hayworths are, but I never had an inkling... are Homeland Security watching them?"

"I wouldn't know," Liane said blandly. Of course, she'd already passed on everything she knew to Homeland Security. Hestia was, after all, named for the goddess of home and hearth. At least eighty per cent of their operating capital came out of Homeland Security's black operations budget. And considering the reaction of her contact when she'd passed on Hayworth's name, she had no doubt there was some serious scrambling going on over there trying to figure out just how radicalized that church had become and what exactly the Hayworths might be planning to do with a suitcase nuke.

Spires ended the video call after a few more questions, and Liane sighed and rubbed at her eyes, leaning back in her office chair. She hadn't slept well since Jessikah left on the mission, worrying about her baby sister's safety.

"I am so damn glad it wasn't you who had to go in undercover on that mission." Drew had been waiting silently in a corner of her office, out of range of the webcam. He came forward now and leaned on the back of her chair, stooping to press a kiss to her forehead.

"I'm not, because Jess is in there instead!" Liane leaned against him, grateful for his warm, solid strength. "I want to be out there *doing* something. Not knowing exactly what's happening is driving me mad. I wonder if we could hack into the CIA's satellite feed, watch in real time?"

"Maybe some of our tech geniuses could, but is that really the best use of our resources? And what would you see, anyway? Little stick figures walking about between buildings, at best. It doesn't give you any real idea of what's going on. Trust me, I got real-time satellite intel plenty of times on missions, and it was more frustrating than useful most of the time."

"You're right." She turned her face against his side, mumbled into the fabric of his T-shirt. "I know you're right. And I know you and I are needed here to run the op from this end, but part of me still wants to be out there in the field."

"Hey." Drew brushed her hair back from her forehead, grinning down at her. "I get it. I want to be storming that island with a team of Rangers and my sniper rifle."

"Maybe we could get to go along on the bust on the Hayworth place," Liane mused, and felt Drew stiffen. His expression, when she looked up at him, was eager.

"Do you think they might let us?"

He missed fieldwork too, she thought. Neither of them were quite reconciled to the fact that they were management now, with desks their battlefields.

"We could always ask. Or just turn up when they're going in for the op." She grinned mischievously up at him.

"It might not get that far," Drew warned. "Might get intercepted at the port of entry. Fortuna might not be as clever as he thinks he is."

"From what DDO Spires said when I told her that Fortuna is really Sebastian Maroney, I think he's very bloody clever indeed. He managed to fake his own death, hide it from the *CIA*, and become one of the world's biggest arms dealers. You really think he can't get a suitcase nuke onto US soil undetected?"

"Fair point," Drew conceded.

"I don't think we're going to know where it is until the date and time of specified delivery to the Hayworths. So that's where it has to be intercepted."

They stared at each other, and Liane knew they were both feeling it. The bubble of rising anticipation at the knowledge that action was coming.

"We're getting in on that bust," Drew said.

"Yes. Yes, we are."

Chapter 17

Neither Jess nor Pascal had been in any kind of mood to either make love for real or even fake it for the audio surveillance. Instead, they curled up together and just lay, not talking. Breathing in quiet unison, anyone listening would probably think they were taking a nap, but both of them were deep in thought, thinking through the consequences of what had happened that afternoon.

At last, Pascal kissed Jess on the forehead and murmured "We should get ready for dinner."

"I suppose." She reached up and kissed him on the lips, thinking even as she pulled away that it had felt completely natural to do so. Lying in Pascal's arms for a couple of hours this afternoon had been some of the most comfortable, peaceful time she could recall spending in a long while. Ever, if she was being completely honest with herself. Yes, at first her mind had whirled with possibilities, with options potentially open to them, with all the ways things might go wrong… but even that had eventually faded away and Jess had found her mind empty of everything but the reassuringly steady thud of Pascal's heart beating beneath her ear. She'd been in a kind of meditative, fugue state when he spoke, startling her.

Pascal's hand curled in her hair, bringing her gently back close so that he could return the kiss, but much hotter and longer. Jess was gasping when he let go, suddenly rethinking their choice of how to spend their time for the last couple of hours. He must have read the regret on her face, because he grinned and chucked her chin lightly.

"Hold that thought for later. I'm hungry."

"Me too… but not for food." She eyed him hungrily as he got up and stretched, thick muscles rippling under brown skin.

"Put your tongue back in." He ran his hands through his hair, dark curls unruly and a shade too long, and winked at her before making for the bathroom.

I shouldn't be letting my libido have free rein. This can't end well. Jess threw herself back against the pillows, frustrated.

She couldn't bring herself to regret having sex with Pascal, though. It had been amazing, and she knew herself well enough to know that she'd take every opportunity to repeat the experience that presented itself. It would be oh-so-easy to get addicted to the way she felt when she was with him, and she didn't just mean in bed.

"So what fabulous dress are you going to wow us with tonight?" Pascal asked, coming out of the bathroom toweling his hair dry.

She smirked. "You'll just have to wait and see."

"Not too long, I hope," he said with a pointed glance at his watch, and Jess sighed, pushing herself up to get out of bed.

"I'll be quick."

Not nearly as quick as she would be if she didn't have the facade of an Instagram model to keep up, but she was still ready in just over half an hour, her face made up and wearing a beautiful pale green silk wrap dress which showed off her long legs but still screamed money and class. As it should, considering what she'd paid for it.

"You look amazing," Pascal murmured, coming up behind her as she checked herself over in the mirror, adding some chunky silver bangles and a pair of earrings with fine dangling chains that brushed her shoulders. He nuzzled the top of her ear gently, his arms slipping around her waist, and in the mirror's reflection Jess saw him close his eyes for a moment, a smile touching his lips as he breathed in her scent.

He feels something too. He doesn't need to be doing that. There's no cameras in here.

She tried hard to stomp on the surging butterflies in her stomach. It was ridiculous to feel like an excited teenager at the smallest sign Pascal might have feelings for her beyond the facade they were being forced to portray.

"Let's go. I'm hungry." Forcing a bright smile, she turned and threaded her arm through his. "Do you think you boys will want to play cards again tonight?"

"Maybe." Pascal shrugged. "Will you deal for us again?"

"Sure. Without Hayworth there to accuse me of dealing from the bottom of the deck and glowering every time I do much as smile, it might even be fun!"

"You don't want to join in and play?"

"No," she said. "I'm terrible at cards."

Pascal gave her a skeptical look, and Jess grinned. That had been a massive lie. She was very, very good at most card games, her photographic memory and math skills giving her an advantage few could match. Though she'd gone through college on a full-ride scholarship, she'd supplemented her income playing online poker, plus a few in-person games where, just as in her professional life, others underestimated her because of the way she looked.

“Remind me never to play poker against you,” he murmured as they left the villa and made their way back to the main resort building.

“I knew you were a smart guy. Slow down a little bit, would you? These heels are the devil to walk in.”

Pascal slowed his stride immediately. “Sorry. Wasn’t paying attention.”

“It’s okay. Normally I’d keep up with you fine.” Jess grimaced. The heels were actually the thing she was finding most difficult about this whole operation; her ankles were hurting constantly and the mere thought of having to run in them was making her twitchy. On the other hand, they were sharp enough to be weapons in a pinch, she consoled herself. Maybe she should engineer a pair with heels that were detachable and actual weapons... she’d had to dispose of the USB key she’d brought in smuggled in a heel, for fear of a search being conducted and it being found. She’d buried it as deep as she could shove it in the sand beneath the villa’s rear deck.

They were nearing the main building when a strange sound off to one side of the path made Jess pause in her step.

"What?" Pascal asked, slowing with her.

"I hear something… I think someone's crying." She unhooked her hand from Pascal's arm and stepped off the path, ignoring his hissed admonition to wait.

"Jess, let me." He grabbed her arm. "You're gonna… yep, there you go."

"Oh, bollocks," she muttered under her breath as her heels sank in the soft grass. "Ugh. Pull me out."

"I got you." He pulled her out, laughing quietly. "Just stand there on the path and let me investigate."

"No need," a choked little voice said, and a small shadow detached from one of the nearby palm trees.

"Mariska," Jess said softly. "Oh, honey. What did he do to you?"

Even in the faint light cast by the torch flames which were all that lit the path, they could see the blackening bruises on the Chechen girl's fair skin.

"He was angry." Mariska's mouth trembled. "Losing the auction."

"And he took it out on you." Jess moved forward, reaching to gingerly put her arm around Mariska's waist. "You poor thing."

"He kick me out." Mariska sagged against Jess. "I don't know what to do..."

"You're going to come to our villa and let me have a look at you, and get some rest." Jess made a snap decision. "Pascal - can you get her something to eat, sugar? She doesn't want to go in there and have to face everyone." She jerked her head towards the main building, and Pascal sighed, obviously seeing the determined look on her face.

"All right. I'll have to tell Fortuna. If Dzhokharov is looking for Mariska, we don't need to get in the middle of it. I can sell you looking after her... for now."

There was a warning note in his voice, and Jess knew that if Dzhokharov demanded Mariska's return, they'd have to give her up, or risk a disaster they couldn't afford. Their mission had to come first, even though her blood was boiling with rage over the Chechen general's cruelty.

"Come on. You come with me." Gently, Jess encouraged Mariska to walk with her, supporting the girl's slight weight. "Can you walk okay, or should I get Pascal to carry you?"

"No, I walk." Mariska bravely took a step, then another, and Jess nodded to Pascal, who took his cue and headed towards the main building.

"You said you help me get away," Mariska whispered as they made slow, painful progress back to the villa. "Did you mean it?"

"Of course. But you understand... I can't get you away from here. I can't even get *us* away from here. No phones."

"Yes. I understand."

They made slow progress. Mariska was obviously in a lot of pain; Jess thought she might have cracked ribs, from the way she was breathing and flinching with every step. Eventually, they made it back to the villa and

Jess guided Mariska gently inside and urged her to lie down on the bed, finally getting a good look at her in decent light and swearing a blue streak under her breath.

A shocking bruise was purpling the entire side of Mariska's face, swelling fast and forcing her left eye almost shut. Blood welled thickly from the corner of her lip, and seeing that, Jess hurried to get some ice and wrap it in a cloth.

"Here. Hold this against your face. I've got ibuprofen here somewhere." She scrabbled among the cosmetics she'd left spread out on the dresser. "Best we can do unless Pascal can talk Fortuna into handing over something stronger."

"Not want stronger." Mariska shook her head, wincing with pain at the unguarded movement. "Stronger... not good."

Confused, Jess frowned at her.

"Stronger mean heroin," Mariska said quietly. "Not want. Seen other girls."

"Oh." Jess wanted to kick herself. Of course. "I won't let them give you heroin. I promise.

But you could take these. They're just Advil. Ibuprofen." She put two tablets into Mariska's hand, grabbed a bottle of water from the refrigerator. "Now. Tell me where else it hurts."

Mariska put a hand to her stomach, wincing, and slowly pulled up her top to show a dark red mark on her stomach.

"Oh jeez, that looks awful." Jess winced in sympathy. "He punched you?"

"Punch me here." Mariska gestured to her face. "When I fall down, he kick me, here." She pointed at her stomach.

For a brief moment, Jess saw red. Debated storming off to find Dzhokharov and giving him a taste of his own medicine. She made herself breathe slowly and deeply, holding her hand out towards Mariska. "Would it be okay if I touched you, here? I want to try and see if you have any broken ribs, because if you do, I think you need a hospital. You probably need a hospital anyway, but..."

"Not be allowed." Mariska shrugged fatalistically. "Mr Fortuna, he not let anyone leave until sale is over. He not care if I die. I not one of the buyers."

"We're not going to let you die." Jess waited for Mariska's nod before probing gently around the younger girl's ribcage. She breathed a quiet sigh of relief when Mariska didn't wince particularly; while the kick to the stomach was obviously painful and now turning all shades of black and purple, Jess didn't think it was a serious injury.

"Lay down," she said quietly, and pulled a coverlet over Mariska as she heard footsteps approaching, and then Pascal came into the villa with a covered tray in his hands. Josef was behind him.

"How badly is the girl hurt?" Josef asked abruptly. He frowned at the sight of Mariska's bruised face and walked forward, bending down to peer at her. She shrank away from him.

"I've given her ibuprofen and an ice pack," Jess said. "Which is about all I can do."

"We could probably find something stronger," Josef said thoughtfully.

“Not want,” Mariska put in quickly. “Not heroin.”

“More likely to be cocaine, here.” He gave her a half-smile. “Or marijuana.”

“Thank you. Not want.”

“Your funeral.” Josef shrugged, obviously not caring one way or the other. “Mr Fortuna appreciates your looking after her,” he turned to address Pascal, “but obviously she can’t stay here. I’ll have her moved while you and the other guests are at dinner.”

“Where to? Not back to Dzhokharov’s villa?” Pascal asked.

“I’ll put her in with the other girls for now. They’ll look after her.”

Jess was pretty sure Josef didn’t care one way or the other, but Fortuna had obviously instructed him to take care of the problem. Likely enough Dzhokharov would be demanding Mariska be returned to him by tomorrow.

“Please, go and have dinner. Thanks for concerning yourselves, but I’ll take it from here.”

Jess didn't particularly want to leave Josef in their villa with Mariska, but Pascal squeezed her arm lightly, and she realized they didn't have much choice. She nodded, bending to Mariska and looking into her eyes.

"When we get out of here," she promised softly. "As *soon* as we get out of here."

"Thank you," Mariska whispered back, reaching to squeeze her hand, and the trust in her one good eye broke Jess's heart, because she didn't know if she'd be able to keep the promise. She didn't know if any of them were going to make it off Isla Fortuna alive, and if she'd ever be able to find Mariska again if they did.

She had no choice but to take Pascal's arm and leave the villa again, hoping desperately that Josef wouldn't hurt Mariska further.

"That poor kid," Pascal muttered. "I want to kill Dzhokharov so badly I can *taste* it."

"You can get in line," Jess said savagely. "He *kicked* Mariska in the stomach!"

"Bastard." Pascal's fists were clenched, his shoulders tight, and Jess felt comforted by his obvious rage, even though the face he'd shown Josef was one of indifference.

"If we get the opportunity," she said, very softly, "let's make sure he doesn't make it to Gitmo."

Pascal glanced sideways at her. "You've changed your tune."

She knew what he meant... but if anyone deserved killing, it was the Chechen who'd bought a teenage girl from her family to satisfy unspeakable lusts and now treated her as his personal punching bag.

Not to mention that Dzhokharov was literally on the island to buy a nuclear weapon which could cause the death of thousands if not millions of people, of course, but what he'd done to Mariska was different, it was up close and personal, not an abstract concept.

Jess no longer doubted her own ability to pull the trigger. If someone had put a gun in her hand right that moment and Dzhokharov in front of her, she wouldn't have hesitated for a second. She was honestly not sure how she was going to sit and eat dinner in the same room without losing her temper.

Apparently reading her mind, Pascal squeezed her hand. “Just don't look at him,” he advised quietly. “Pretend he's not there. I've had to sit down with some truly appalling individuals over the years; you have to learn to set it aside.”

She took a deep breath of the warm, hibiscus-and-salt scented night air, and nodded. “I'll try.”

“Just remember why we're here.” He squeezed her hand again. “You can do it.”

The words were said with such calm conviction, Jess immediately felt steadier. Pascal's faith in her was heart-warming, especially considering that he'd only known her a few days. “I won't let you down,” she said softly as they entered the main building, heading for the dining room.

“Take comfort in knowing that I want to kill him just as much as you do!”

Pascal's muttered remark made her chuckle, and both of them managed to have a smile on their faces as they joined the rest of the party.

Chapter 18

Pascal was proud of the way Jess managed to conduct herself during the dinner, especially with Dzhokharov being loud and obnoxiously drunk across the table. The Chechen was clearly still in a bad mood after losing out at the auction earlier, and getting stuck deep into the vodka - deep enough to indiscreetly admit that his top bid had only been sufficient to earn him fourth place.

Which meant, Pascal suspected after Fortuna's sniping at Breukel earlier, that the Dutchman's bid had been the low one. And with Pascal's bid having been third, that put the North Koreans in as the runners-up.

Yoon was sitting with his head close together with Doctor Choe, the pair of them ignoring the rest of the company as they talked quietly, despite one of Fortuna's girls sitting on Yoon's lap. Somehow, Pascal didn't think the Koreans were going to be sharing how much their bid had been, but it was very possible Dzhokharov might, especially if he consumed much more vodka. And that could be very useful information to have.

"Get our friend here another drink," he said to Jess as Dzhokharov slammed his empty glass down on the table with a scowl. "Are you up for another game of poker tonight, General?"

"*Da!*" Dzhokharov laughed boisterously, reaching out to pat Jess's ass as she stood beside his chair to pour more vodka into his glass. "You good girl," he said. "Not like my silly little wife."

Jess had managed to hold herself admirably still and not react to the pat, but she stiffened now. "Your *wife*?" she said, tone icy.

"*Da*, Mariska. Foolish child. Ran off this afternoon. Not that she can go far, not on an island, eh?" Dzhokharov chuckled a deep belly laugh and nudged Fortuna. "She come back. Maybe in the morning. Won't hurt her to miss dinner."

Pascal saw Jess look at the bottle in her hand and just knew she was considering braining the Chechen with it. He caught her eye and shook his head infinitesimally.

Jess sighed and set the bottle down. "Can I get anyone else anything?" she asked sweetly.

Breukel asked for another beer, but everyone else declined and Jess returned to her seat beside Pascal a moment later. Instead of letting her sit down, he hooked an arm around her waist and pulled her into his lap, nuzzling his face against her neck. She was tense against him, clearly fighting down rage, but slowly began to relax as he stroked his hand down her spine. Finally he felt her heave a small sigh and turn her face against his cheek.

"I'm okay," she whispered, under the guise of nibbling on his earlobe.

"I know. You got this. Just keep it together." He kissed her lips lightly, gave her a meaningful look, and reached for a platter of chocolate-coated strawberries on the table, bringing one to her lips.

Jess bit into the strawberry, giving Pascal a deliberately sultry look, and he smiled, feeling his body react. She obviously felt it too, because she wiggled against him and gave a quiet little laugh.

"Behave, minx." He squeezed the nape of her neck lightly, then said in a conversational tone, "Go get the cards, Jess. Let's see if we can have a decent game tonight without that amateur Hayworth not having a clue when he's even got a decent hand."

Everyone laughed at that, and Jessikah obediently got to her feet. Josef was quick to produce the cards and the piles of printed slips they were using in place of actual money again, and Jess shuffled deftly.

"You never did say which variant of poker you played last night," she noted. "Texas Hold'Em?"

"Yes, we played that last night," Breukel answered. "It was the only kind of poker Hayworth had ever seen - watched some on TV. I'd rather seven card stud. Anyone else?"

"Fine by me," Fortuna said with a shrug. He seemed preoccupied this evening, occasionally checking his phone. Pascal guessed Fortuna was busy arranging the transportation of Hayworth's nuke; he doubted any of the devices were on US soil and getting it in would likely not be simple logistically. He burned to get a look at that phone, but short of killing every man in the room and wrestling the phone from Fortuna's corpse he couldn't really see how it might be done.

"Do you know how to deal seven-card stud, angel?" Pascal asked Jess, who was deftly shuffling the cards.

"Sure. Daddy likes to play it with his buddies in Val d'Isère." Her hands flashed, dealing each of the men two cards face down, one card face up. "Looks like you've the low card, Mr Yoon."

The North Korean was already pushing a single slip to the center of the table; Breukel, seated beside him, couldn't check and was forced to bet too. Pascal edged his cards up with his thumb to check them, wrinkled his nose and decided to fold. Hopeless. The eight showing face up was the best card he had, and none of them were even the same suit. Well, there was always the next round. And a few dozen more after that, if the previous evening was any guide.

Fortuna was a very good poker player, and so was Yoon, if a little cautious. Pascal suspected that Breukel was underplaying his skills, as Pascal was himself, not wanting to give himself away. Dzhokharov, however, was reckless, and lost far more often than he won because he didn't seem to be able to bring himself to fold, no matter how bad his cards were.

About an hour into the game, they were briefly interrupted when one of the girls came into the room and spoke quietly to Josef, whose face darkened. He gestured the girl to stay put before coming up behind Fortuna and bending to whisper in his ear.

"At the end of this game," was all Fortuna said, not even looking around, but when the game ended he looked up and pinned Dzhokharov with a glare. "You said your wife ran off, Ruslan. You didn't say you'd beaten her up."

"Beat her up." The Chechen shrugged insouciantly. "Is nothing. She is my wife. Discipline is essential."

"She's pissing blood, according to Camila." Fortuna gestured to the girl who'd come in; Pascal remembered the name. The girl Hayworth had abused on the first night. She stood in the shadows at the back of the room, but he could see the bruising darkening one side of her face, as well as the anger on it as she looked at Dzhokharov.

"You asshole!" Jess obviously lost her temper, rising to her feet. "She's just a kid..."

Dzhokharov's face darkened, and he stood too, raising his fist. "You *dare* speak to me, woman!"

"That's enough." Fortuna moved smoothly between the two. "Isla Fortuna Continental is a sanctuary, remember? Violence is not permitted towards your fellow guests."

"Apparently your sanctuary doesn't extend to Mariska... or Camila," Pascal said dryly, and Dzhokharov turned a killing glare on him. Pascal didn't care, he had to get the Chechen's attention off Jess. "You talk a big game,

Fortuna, but so far nobody seems to have suffered any consequences for breaching your rules."

Fortuna went very still, staring at Pascal, and for just an instant his affable mask of politeness slipped and Pascal saw the psychopath beneath.

"You're right," Fortuna said after a moment of absolute stillness which seemed to stretch for an eternity. "You're absolutely right, Montalban. It's too late to discipline Hayworth, regrettably, but Ruslan... you have shown a distinct disrespect for the sanctuary of Isla Fortuna. You may consider this your only warning."

"And what if I breach your foolish rules again?" Dzhokharov swelled his chest, his face turning red.

"You will not be permitted to bid at the remaining auctions," Fortuna said blandly.

"Is not fair - I paid the buy-in!" Dzhokharov was starting to whine.

Pascal had to wonder when was the last time someone had presented Dzhokharov with negative consequences of his actions. The Chechen seemed stunned; disbelieving.

"Mariska is my *wife*!"

"She's fourteen," Pascal said quickly, seeing Jess open her mouth.

"Wait. Fourteen?" Even Fortuna looked a little queasy about that. "You brought a fourteen-year-old girl to my island..."

"My *wife*!" Dzhokharov exclaimed.

"Your wife, who's pissing blood because you kicked her in the stomach," Jess snapped.

Dzhokharov's fists clenched, and Pascal didn't try to hold back the instinctive growl that erupted from him as Dzhokharov turned back towards Jess.

"Gentlemen." Fortuna gestured, and Josef was suddenly holding a gun, pointed at Dzhokharov.

Josef moved way faster than Pascal had expected, and he almost reacted very badly indeed. From the corner of his eye he saw Breukel twitch his hand towards his belt, obviously aborting reaching for his weapon when he realized he didn't have it.

"Ruslan. Please go to your villa," Fortuna said into the tense silence. "I will see to it that your wife receives medical attention for the duration of your stay on the island."

For a moment, Pascal thought Dzhokharov was going to argue, but the Chechen looked at the gun in Josef's hand and made a growling noise in his throat before turning and stalking out of the room. Josef followed at a nod from Fortuna.

"Do you have someone with medical training on your staff?" Jess asked.

Fortuna turned to give her a sharp look. "Nobody who has more than a basic first aid certificate. And no, I am not going to recruit and fly in someone just for the girl. I'm sorry, but I cannot risk bringing in an unvetted stranger at this late date - nor can I allow her to leave the island unless her life is in imminent danger. If you want to check on her, I have no objection to your doing that... as long as Ruslan doesn't see you doing it. I don't think he'll be pleased and I'd prefer you don't antagonize him further."

Pascal caught Jess's eye, gave a subtle, warning shake of his head. She took a visible breath, pasted on a smile and said; "Oh that's so sweet of you, Mr Fortuna, and I will, if you really don't mind. Mariska's a sweet little thing and she don't deserve to be treated like that."

"Camila will take you to see her." Fortuna flicked a hand in the other girl's direction. "Soraya. Take over the dealing, will you? I'm on a hot streak. No need to stop the game just because one player's out."

Jess glanced at Pascal, and he gave a small nod, indicating that she should leave. She was angry and might say something unwise if she stayed, potentially raising Fortuna's suspicions again. She nodded and came around the table to kiss him farewell.

"I'll see you back at our villa later," she murmured.

"You be waiting when I get back." He made a show of lazily patting her ass, and she laughed softly and left, following Camila.

“Your woman’s too kind for this life,” Breukel said unexpectedly, looking at Pascal. “Got compassion. Rare, for a trust fund type.”

“She’s gonna see much worse than Dzhokharov, if she sticks with you,” Fortuna muttered, checking his cards as Soraya dealt the new hand. “She needs to learn how to hide her emotions - and how to lie worth a damn. I could tell she wanted to smack me for not getting medical treatment for the girl, but she pasted on that smile and thanked me sweetly. She’s lucky I like you both.” He glanced up, met Pascal’s gaze, and gave him a wintry smile. “And that child brides are one of the few lines I won’t cross. Dzhokharov is a pig.”

“He is,” Pascal agreed. “I’ve dealt with him before and he’s not just lacking in moral compass - let’s face it, if any of us had moral compasses, we wouldn’t be here - he takes active pleasure in cruelty. It’s wasteful and unnecessary.”

“Exactly.” Fortuna pointed at him, included Breukel, Dr Choe and Mr Yoon as he gestured around the table. “We’re pragmatists. Dzhokharov and Hayworth? Fanatics.”

Pascal nodded in agreement, folding his hand and leaning back in his chair, affecting casualness. "You're right. We have to deal with them, but we don't have to like them."

"Just to pretend we do," Breukel said dryly.

"Thank you for understanding that we are not also fanatics," Dr Choe said, after Yoon spoke rapidly to her. "We are working in the service of our country. There is no higher calling. Personal wants and desires cannot interfere with what we must do."

"Of course," Fortuna said, but he glanced at Pascal again, his mouth twisting wryly, and Pascal knew the arms dealer didn't mean a word of it. "Come on, Dieter. Are you in or not?"

"Not. It's rubbish." Breukel threw his hand in, ceding the pot to Fortuna. "Go again, Soraya, and try and give me something to work with this time!"

Chapter 19

Jess followed Camila out of the main resort building and down a path which wasn't as well lit as the one to her and Pascal's villa. She remembered one of the girls saying they shared a villa, when they weren't required to entertain the guests, but the building Camila led her to was more like a dormitory, and Jess guessed it had been exactly that, for staff when the resort was open for paying customers.

Mariska was lying on a bed just inside the door, curled in the fetal position. She was silent, but when Jess crouched down beside her she could see tears on the younger girl's cheeks.

"Are you in a lot of pain?" Jess asked quietly.

Mariska seemed to think about her words for a few moments, perhaps struggling to find the English to express herself. “I have hurt worse,” she said finally.

“Camila said there was blood in your urine. When you went to the toilet,” Jess clarified when Mariska looked puzzled.

“Not so much. A little pink, only. Camila is fussing.” Mariska shrugged, then winced, the movement obviously paining her. “I will be better tomorrow.”

Camila had been standing silently by, watching; at Mariska’s words she sighed loudly. “You *not* better tomorrow. Bruises worse the day after.” Turning away, she went to a fridge at the other end of the room, came back with some ice wrapped in a cloth. “Here. Put this on your eye. We can help that.”

Mariska took the cloth and pressed it to her swollen eye, and Camila nodded, retreating to what was apparently her own bed at the other end of the room. Mariska glanced up at Jess from her good eye, then hesitantly gestured at the side of the bed.

“You like to sit down?”

Jess sat down, reached tentatively to stroke Mariska's hair. The Chechen girl seemed to find a little comfort in the gentle touch, moving closer and sighing quietly.

"Dzhokharov said you were his wife," Jess said very quietly.

Mariska stiffened, and then she nodded. "Da. Is true."

"You didn't tell me that earlier."

"I thought... you offered to help me. But is different, for a man's wife. I thought you might not, if you knew."

"You were wrong. I'll help you."

Mariska peered at her for a moment, lifted her head to look across the room to Camila, who was wearing headphones plugged into what looked like an old cassette tape deck and nodding along, apparently to music.

Very quietly, Mariska whispered; "You CIA?"

Jess blinked. "No," she said, knowing immediately that she'd spoken a little too quickly. "What makes you think that?"

"Rich girl not care what happens to girls like me. And - I saw you. With computers."

Jess knew what Mariska meant. The Chechen girl had indeed seen her in the server room, a place where Jess not only had no business but was absolutely forbidden to be.

"I'm not CIA," she whispered, leaning down close under the guise of closely inspecting Mariska's eye. "I'm something else. Please believe me, Pascal and I can help you escape Dzhokharov. He'll never find you."

"I help you," Mariska said unexpectedly. "And then you help me. Da?"

"Sure." Jess regarded Mariska curiously. "How is it you think you can help me?"

"I tell you what Dzhokharov bid at the auction. He not want to spend all the money he has been given to pay, wanted to keep some for himself, but he know now that he have to. Fourth in auction not good enough. Politicians who send him be very angry."

"I've been wondering," Jess said delicately, wondering how much she dared say. Wondering if Fortuna would have bothered to bug this villa. *Why would he?* He thought the only people who would be in here were the sex workers he'd hired to entertain his guests. "Why Chechnya are even bidding for this weapon?"

Mariska's smile was weary. "Is not Chechnya - not officially. Not president and his government. Other faction. Think Russians should not be in Chechnya."

"Oh," Jess said softly, shocked. "So if they get the weapon..."

"Use it in false flag operation to start war between Russia and NATO. Then make coup in Chechnya and break free of Russia."

"Holy shit." In the back of her mind, Jess had wondered if it was something like that, but to hear it laid out so baldly - the Chechen separatists were planning to start World War III to reclaim their country, and Dzhokharov must be very highly placed in the ranks of the would-be rebels. It threw into sharp relief the dangers of these nukes getting into the wrong hands, and the critical importance of their mission here.

More important than one child bride, though she hated to admit it. Still, her kindness to Mariska was producing real, tangible results, with the intelligence the girl was providing.

"So," Jess murmured, stroking Mariska's hair tenderly. "How much?"

"He bid twelve and a half. Budget is twenty," Mariska whispered back. "He cannot spend more than that. They do not have it, and Fortuna must be paid at once."

"I understand."

Mariska didn't ask what Pascal had bid, which convinced Jess that she was telling the truth, that she wasn't trying to pump Jess for information in return by eliciting sympathy. Frankly, she didn't think the girl had it in her to be deceitful. She was young, barely educated, and extremely resentful of her situation. She had every incentive to try and escape her abusive older husband, and Jess was likely the first person she'd ever met who'd given her even a glimmer of hope that there might be a way out.

"Thank you for your help," Jess said quietly. "I promise I'll do everything in my power to help you too, when the time comes."

Mariska nodded, her eyelids drooping. Jess reached to pull the coverlet over her.

"Get some sleep, kiddo. I'll come check on you in the morning."

Pascal was late to bed; Jess was already asleep when he got back to the villa, tired and edgy from having to watch every word and every gesture. Crawling into bed beside her, he lay awake, trying to ease the tension in his muscles enough to fall asleep. He failed utterly... at least until she sighed and rolled over in her sleep, throwing an arm across his chest, her cheek pressing against his shoulder.

The proximity, the soft warmth of her relaxed, sleeping body beside him, helped something unknot in him and finally, he drifted off to sleep.

He woke in the early morning light, aware that something wasn't right; it took a few seconds for him to realize it was the absence of Jess which disturbed him. She slipped back into bed a minute later, murmuring apology. "Had to go to the bathroom. Go back to sleep. It's early."

Pascal was wide awake now, though, and he sensed Jess was too, by her shallow breathing. Almost absently, he reached out and cupped her shoulder; she rolled closer and rested her cheek on his bicep.

"Can't sleep?" she asked quietly.

"No. Thinking about the next auction. Fortuna hinted he might move it up to today, instead of making us wait until tomorrow. He can see Dzhokharov is antsy, and Breukel too."

"Mm." She hesitated a moment, then said delicately "I've been having second thoughts about who Breukel might be working for. If your theory is right... wouldn't his budget be effectively infinite?"

Like us, was the unspoken subtext. Pascal turned his head to look at her, frowning. "So who do you think he's working for?" he asked.

"I don't know. He's a blank slate, and it bothers me."

He'd thought from the beginning that Jess seemed to have good instincts. If she thought Breukel might be a problem, then Pascal needed to pay closer attention to the Dutch middleman. He admitted to himself that he'd dismissed Breukel because he thought he knew the other man, knew what to expect from him. Breukel and Yoon had taken less of his attention, because Fortuna was a dangerous unknown and Hayworth and Dzhokharov were loose cannons.

The simple fact was, he couldn't afford to take his eye off any of the multiple balls all up in the air at the same time. While he hadn't gone so far as to assume Breukel really was working for Interpol or another security agency, in the back of his mind Pascal had written the Dutchman off as a serious threat, and that was unwise. Jess's words were a sharp reminder that he could trust literally no one apart from the woman lying beside him.

"How was Mariska?" He changed the subject, not wanting to dwell overmuch on his own sloppiness. *Maybe it really is time I got out of the field*.

“Sore, but I think she’ll heal,” Jess said, her mouth twisting down at the corners. “I’m sure in a hospital they’d send her for all sorts of scans and tests, but I don’t think there’s a lot they would actually do for her beyond pain relief.”

“Poor kid,” Pascal murmured.

“She let slip an interesting nugget of information,” Jess said, and Pascal could tell she was being cautious with her words. “Something you might like to know. Turns out Dzhokharov isn’t here on behalf of the Chechen government. He’s buying on behalf of a separatist movement.”

“Oh?” That was interesting information. Pascal hadn’t had any inkling Dzhokharov wasn’t completely sanctioned.

“Mm hm. They’re planning to use the weapon in a false flag op to start a war between Russia and NATO, then declare independence while the Russians are otherwise occupied.”

Pascal let out a low whistle. “That’s... ambitious.”

“*Insane* was the word I had in mind. But I guess, if you back someone into a corner hard enough, the only way out they can see is to knock down the whole damn house.” Jess shrugged. “Anyway, I don’t think they have the money. Mariska said they have an absolute cap of twenty million. Dzhokharov bid twelve... she seems to think he planned to salt a chunk away for his own purposes if he could, but now he realizes he’ll have to bid the whole lot to be in with a shot.”

“Yeah, he’s out of the running in that case. I have more than that to work with, and I’m pretty sure Yoon does too.”

“So, assuming that Dzhokharov and Breukel are the low bids,” Jess pointed out, “what do you think they’ll do after we leave? Do you think Fortuna will have something else to offer them - some sort of consolation prize?”

He seriously hoped not. But it would be just like Fortuna to do that - the arms dealer wouldn’t want money left on the table. Maybe he’d have something less flashy than a suitcase nuke but potentially just as lethal. A chemical or bio-weapon, for example.

"I'll try and nudge Fortuna. See if he'll tell me anything," Pascal murmured.

"Otherwise, I guess the only way we'd find out is if we lose the second and third auction." Jess held his gaze, and he winced, but nodded, seeing her point. She was absolutely correct. They needed to stay on the island after the end of the last auction to find out what else Fortuna was up to.

It was risky. Especially since they had to put complete trust in the teams working on the outside, to intercept the weapons - and he had to put total blind faith in Jess's worm actually delivering the intel in time for that to happen. Plus, if Fortuna got wind of the weapons being intercepted before delivery, he might well start looking at just how the information was leaking. Pascal and Jess could be trapped on the island with a furious Fortuna looking for a scapegoat.

"Let's worry about that when the time comes," he said finally.

Jess nodded. She snuggled closer to him, tracing her fingers lightly across his collarbones, down his chest. Over the tattoo on his left pectoral muscle. “A raven?” she murmured.

“I like them. Clever birds.” It didn’t hold any special meaning for him, but he’d had it done because a man in his profession without some ink would be rare enough to occasion comment.

“I like them too.”

Her light touch was starting to arouse him; he glanced a quick apology as his rising cock brushed her thigh.

She grinned and reached down. “Well hello there.”

“Hello yourself,” he said gruffly, and groaned as she slid down the bed and opened her mouth over him.

Jess’s mouth was hot and knowing, her deft hands cupping his balls and curving around the base of his shaft, and it was scant seconds before he was rock hard and desperate to be inside her. Determined not to rush things, he ran his hands into her hair and tugged lightly, pulling her mouth off his cock and bringing her torso up flush with his again.

"I want you," he muttered roughly against her mouth, and she nodded, twining herself around him and gasping with pleasure as his hands closed on her breasts.

"Yes," she agreed. "*Yes*."

She was as hungry as he, Pascal thought as she matched his urgency, her slim body arching against his, cries of pleasure spilling from her lips. As desperate as she to escape the difficult dangerous situation they were in, even if it was only a temporary reprieve to lose themselves in the pleasures of the flesh. It was still exactly what he needed.

As they lay together afterwards, sweating and sated, Jess idly tracing the outstretched wings of the raven tattoo on his chest, it hit Pascal that he was going to miss having Jess around when this mission was over. He'd gotten so comfortable with her in the last few days, come to trust her absolutely and also rely on her judgment when he was questioning his own. He smiled slightly, thinking of how he'd utterly misjudged her on their first meeting. He was willing to bet at least part of the eclectic appearance she'd presented was purposefully intended to make people underestimate her.

"You're not at all like I thought you were when we first met," Jess murmured, echoing his own thoughts so precisely he laughed aloud.

"Funny enough, I was just thinking the exact same thing." He flicked a long strand of golden hair in his fingers, dancing the end of it over her bare shoulder. "But then, I think you were deliberately going for shock value."

"Maybe a little. And I thought you were just another suit with no imagination whatsoever." She leaned up on one elbow and gave him a wicked little grin. "I'm glad to have been proved wrong."

Chapter 20

Pascal and Jess made their way to the main building an hour or so later in search of breakfast, finding it almost deserted apart from a few staff members. Everyone else was sleeping in today, it seemed. Josef turned up part-way through their meal and Jess asked if she might go to see Mariska again, figuring this was one case where it was definitely better to ask permission than forgiveness.

"If you wish." Josef gave her a curt nod. He appeared preoccupied, and when Jess had left, Pascal delicately asked Josef if something was troubling him.

Josef shrugged. "Mr Fortuna isn't pleased," he said finally. "Dzhokharov is kicking up a stink about being confined to his villa, but he must understand; he disrespected Mr Fortuna's rules."

"Ah." Fortuna didn't want to kick the Chechen off the island, Pascal surmised, because it would likely reduce the bidding for the remaining nukes. "I have a question," he said, "which you might not be able to answer, but... I was wondering if Mr Fortuna had any sort of consolation prize to offer those bidders who don't manage to purchase one of the devices?"

"What makes you ask that?" Josef said, too quickly and too defensively.

Pascal just shrugged. "It's what I'd do."

"Of course." Josef's glance turned assessing. "You too are a broker, not an end client. I forget. Who is your client, again?"

Pascal laughed.

Josef grinned. "You cannot blame a man for trying. Just as I do not blame you for trying to pump me about Mr Fortuna's business."

"Fair enough." Pascal inclined his head. "I was just curious. Even if I'm not able to complete this transaction on behalf of my client... I would not want to have completely wasted my time here. Especially since the deposit was non-refundable, and came out of my own pocket."

"I do not think you will leave disappointed," Josef said, and Pascal figured that was as strong a hint as he was going to get, that Fortuna did indeed have something else up his sleeve to offer the losing buyers after the auctions were concluded.

Damn. Jess was right.

However, he now had the information he needed to ensure he lost the third auction, because he knew Dzhokharov had twenty million to spend. If Pascal bid just a little lower than that, he'd lose without it looking obvious that he was trying to.

Assuming Yoon had more than twenty million and was going to win the second auction, that was. All the different variables were making Pascal's head hurt. He downed the last of his coffee with a grimace, just as Fortuna walked in, Soraya on his arm.

"Good morning," Pascal greeted.

Fortuna acknowledged him with a nod, before addressing Josef in rapid-fire Spanish, asking whether Dzhokharov had quietened down.

Pascal poured himself more coffee and sipped it placidly, not allowing his face to show any indication that he was following every word of the conversation. Soraya sat down beside him and leaned in close, obviously intending to draw his gaze to her impressive bosom. He gave her a bland smile and offered to pour her a cup of coffee.

"Fine. Get them all together," Fortuna told Josef, still in that rapid-fire, colloquial Spanish. "We'll do it after breakfast. I'm sick of looking at the whole lot of them. Should have done the whole thing over the web."

Josef left, and Fortuna snapped his fingers for the wait staff, who scurried over to take his order for poached eggs on sourdough with a side of maple bacon.

"Where's Jessica?" Fortuna finally turned his attention to Pascal, a frown creasing his brow slightly as he saw how solicitously close Soraya was sitting. Soraya obviously noticed and hastily put a little distance between herself and Pascal.

"She asked Josef if she could go check up on Mariska. She's got a soft heart, has taken a liking to the kid." Pascal shrugged as though unconcerned.

"Hm." Fortuna drummed his fingers on the table.

"Has Hayworth received his device yet?" Pascal changed the subject, keeping his tone casual. "He doesn't seem the sort to patiently wait for it."

"Tomorrow." Fortuna unbent enough to reveal the little snippet of information, a smug smile creasing his lips. "I knew what sort of budget they were playing with - he offered me an astonishing amount of money to sell him a device without coming to the auction, so I arranged to have one of them pre-positioned in the US so that I could deliver it quickly. A customer with that kind of budget, well." He shrugged.

"You do what you need to in order to keep them happy. Do you really think he'll be a repeat customer, though? I can't imagine their little cult being able to topple enough of the American government to escape consequences." Pascal was genuinely curious whether Fortuna still felt any loyalty at all to the nation of his birth.

"I really don't care whether he comes back or not. And if they do succeed in the destabilization they have planned, I think there will be a lot more buyers looking for all sorts of equipment. More business for both of us." Fortuna toasted Pascal with his coffee cup.

Pascal made himself smile appreciatively, covering his instinctive recoil of revulsion. "I don't suppose you know Hayworth's timeframe? We'd planned to route home back to Europe via the US, perhaps visit Jess's parents, but I'm rethinking that. Might change our plans."

"I would if I were you." Fortuna's gaze was flat. Unblinking. "Might be a good time for Jess's parents to take a European holiday, too."

"Duly noted," Pascal murmured, as Fortuna's breakfast was delivered and the arms dealer turned his attention to his plate. "Well, I think I'll go find Jess. Maybe take a swim."

"Don't go anywhere." Fortuna pointed his fork at Pascal. "We're going to hold the second auction right after I'm done eating."

"Oh. Change of plans? What about the third auction?"

"I'll decide on that later today. Maybe we'll do it tomorrow. Depends on who wins today and where I have to have the second device delivered." Fortuna smirked. "You going to tell me where you'd like it delivered, if you're the high bidder?"

"I'd actually need to consult with my client," Pascal said smoothly. "I'm only authorized to bid on their behalf, not privy to their operational plans."

"Humph." Fortuna turned his attention to his food, cutting up his bacon almost angrily, cutlery rattling against his plate. "Should never have let you and Breukel in here," he muttered. "I like knowing who I'm dealing with."

“Come now.” Pascal worked to make his tone affable. “It’s just business. In our game, middlemen are the norm. Look at who’s made trouble for you here - Hayworth and Dzhokhovic - two of your three end buyers, hm? Whereas Dieter and I are professionals, like you.”

“You’re nothing like me,” Fortuna said flatly.

A tense silence fell. Soraya looked between the two of them, eyes wide; Pascal felt a visceral shudder run up his spine, though he made himself stay absolutely still and held Fortuna’s gaze.

The silence was broken as the door swung open to admit Breukel, Yoon and Dr Choe, none of whom looked particularly happy to be summoned so peremptorily, but were at least more cheerful than Dzhokhorov. The Chechen was puce, muttering under his breath and stamping his feet when he arrived a couple of minutes later.

“We’re holding the auction now.” Fortuna cut off everyone’s protests, throwing down his napkin and getting to his feet. “Josef. The tablets.”

Jess isn't here, Pascal thought as he accepted a tablet from Josef, and she probably wouldn't be allowed in now, with the doors closed and Josef stationing himself in front of them after handing out the tablets. It didn't really matter, though. Pascal knew what his strategy had to be. If Pascal bid no higher than he had the first time around, it would signal to Fortuna that he was at his limit and had been from the start, implying he was being open about his total budget. Presenting himself as exactly what Fortuna expected to see.

Fortuna didn't bother with the theatrics this time around. Five minutes later the auction was over and Yoon and Fortuna were shaking hands, both all smiles. Dzhokharov was looking cautiously pleased; Pascal surmised the Chechen had finally entered his true high bid and come up second, since Pascal's screen displayed a number 3.

Which meant Breukel, currently stalking out of the room with a face like thunder, was the low bidder yet again... and Pascal was definitely leaning more towards Jess's conclusion that Breukel wasn't with Interpol or any other security agency.

Josef collected the tablets again and Fortuna left the room with Yoon and Dr Choe; Dzhokharov sat down at the table and snapped at Soraya to pour him some coffee. She jumped to obey, and Pascal got up to leave, concluding his presence was only likely to aggravate the Chechen further.

"You do not stay to drink coffee with me?" Dzhokharov grumbled.

"I already had my breakfast, Ruslan." Pascal sat back down, though, nodding to Soraya and pointing to his cup. "Are you bored or something?"

"Ha. This bread, is no good. Why is bread in the Americas always so bad?" Dzhokharov poked at the bread roll on his plate. "Should have brought good Chechen bread with me."

"It'd be stale by now," Pascal pointed out. "I agree with you about the bread, though. I think it's the flour. Different wheat varietals in Europe, or something. I'd give a lot for a decent baguette from my local bakery in Marseilles right now."

"That where you actually live, is it?" Dzhokharov gave him a cunning glance.

Pascal shrugged nonchalantly. “As much as I can be said to live anywhere. I own an apartment there, but truthfully, I’m lucky to spend thirty nights a year sleeping in my own bed.” It was a CIA-owned property, of course; he thought that he should pay a visit there again soon. He hadn’t been in six months, and anyone watching might wonder why. Pascal Montalban was on any number of international watch lists, though the CIA ensured no security agencies ever got around to acting on any information anyone might think they had on him.

“And I thought being a soldier kept me from home a lot.” The Chechen snorted, shoveling scrambled eggs into his mouth. “Now I do not even have my wife to keep me company.”

“She’s a child. Why would you bother, when you could have a lovely woman like this one to warm your bed? Our host has been very generous.” Pascal nodded towards Soraya, who preened a little.

“Is fair point. You want to come keep company with me today?” Dzhokharov asked Soraya. “Maybe bring one of your friends with you." He smiled lecherously. "Keep me from getting bored."

"Would you like that?" Soraya purred, leaning in to show Dzhokharov a great view of her spectacular cleavage. "You like to watch?"

"Da, very much. Why don't you come join in, Pascal? Bring that pretty Jess with you."

This was what Dzhokharov really wanted, Pascal surmised at once; the invitation to him was superfluous. Dzhokharov wanted to fuck Jess, and he figured getting them to join in an orgy was his best shot at it.

"I don't share," Pascal said, and he didn't bother to hide the menace in his voice. "Business is business, but what's mine is mine, and that includes Jess. Don't ask again. I wouldn't want to have to take offense."

Honestly sick of the sight of the Chechen, he pushed his chair back and rose to his feet, leaving the dining room without a backward glance. He needed to clear his head, so turned away from the path that led back to the villa, heading down towards the beach.

Jess found him there half an hour later, pacing at the edge of the water. She took her shoes off, joined him and walked in silence for a while.

"What happened?" she asked quietly at last.

"Second auction. Yoon won it. I was third, behind Dzhokharov."

"Huh." Jess nodded, obviously thinking through what had happened. "Guess that's who the chopper is coming in for." She nodded out to sea, and Pascal turned to look. She'd seen it first, the distant speck of the helicopter approaching, and now he could hear the *whup-whup* of its blades over the wind and the waves.

"I just hope your worm worked and our people on the outside are getting the information they need," he said under his breath, watching the helicopter's approach. "Because if not, we're letting nukes go out into the world with no real idea exactly where they're going to end up."

"Have a little faith." Jess slipped her hand into his, squeezed gently. "I made sure the server I set up to receive on the other end pinged back. Every bit of data that was in the island's computers at that point copied itself over, and even if they shut it down after that - which I can't imagine they have because Fortuna would have kicked up a stink by now - my people would have enough information on the buyers to start digging into their finances and following the money."

He sighed, blew out his cheeks. Nodded. "How's Mariska?" he asked after they'd walked in silence for another minute or two.

"Feeling a little better after a decent night's sleep. Camila had brought her some breakfast and she was eating."

"That's good." He looked out to sea. "Jess... Dzhokharov is going to win the third auction. I have to let him, because we need to know what other cards Fortuna is holding."

"I know," she said, brow furrowing as he gave her a meaningful look.

Pascal saw the moment she realized what he was getting at. Her cheeks flushed, her jaw clenched.

"He's going to leave and take Mariska with him, and there's nothing we can do about it," he said gently. "She'll likely be back in Chechnya with him before we even get off this island."

"And we might not be able to get her out." Jess nearly spat the words, her fingers tightening on his. "Shit. I promised I'd help her if I could."

"*If* you could," Pascal pointed out, quiet but merciless. "She'll be far from the only innocent casualty if we can't get the job done here."

"Just the only one I know personally." Jess didn't say anything else for a few minutes, looking at the waves washing over their bare feet as they walked. "I'm really not cut out for this field work thing," she admitted then, glancing sideways up at him. "I was nearly ready then to jeopardize everything for Mariska's sake."

"The trolley problem is horrifying in the abstract. When it's a real-world choice between one person you know and who knows how many faceless strangers, a lot of people freeze. You've got good instincts. You didn't need me to tell you what choice we have to make. I only brought it up to make sure you'd considered it and weren't going to react badly in the heat of the moment if it occurred to you late." He let go of her hand and put his arm around her shoulders, leaning in to press a kiss to the side of her brow. "You're wrong about not being cut out for field work. You haven't put a foot wrong since we got here, and this is very much being thrown in at the deep end."

"Thanks." She leaned against him briefly. "How much longer, do you think? Fortuna's obviously running out of patience. Do you think he'll hold the third auction today?"

"Maybe. He'll need to set some stuff in motion to get Yoon's device delivered, might keep him busy for the rest of the day. We'll just have to wait and see."

Chapter 21

Pascal was on edge the rest of the day, fully expecting the summons at any moment to go to the third and final auction, but it never came. The helicopter took off again as he and Jess were walking back to their villa, flying over low enough for them to see the two North Koreans looking out the side windows in their direction.

"In theory, that should be the easiest to intercept. Probably the one with the longest lead time in it, too," Pascal said quietly. "It'll have to be delivered via ship, and I don't see Fortuna having it literally sitting in a container ship off the Korean coast."

"Let's just hope the Navy are able to do their jobs without stirring up a Chinese shitstorm,"

Jess murmured, shading her eyes as she watched the helicopter flying away.

"That's why we have covert operatives and submarines, Jess. If there's no other alternative, the ship will suffer a fatal malfunction and wind up on the bottom of the ocean." It wouldn't be the preferred outcome - the Israelis almost certainly wanted their missing devices back in their own hands - but it was better than the North Koreans getting their hands on a suitcase nuke to reverse engineer.

They were called for dinner at the usual time, to discover that Fortuna seemed to have recovered his bonhomie and was being charming and genial again.

"So when's the last auction going to be?" Pascal tried a direct question, when there was a brief pause in the chatter. "Tonight? We can get it all over with, and go home."

"Why the hurry?" It was Breukel who asked, the Dutchman's eyes cunning. "I'm enjoying the vacation."

"Sure... but if your clients are anything like mine, the sooner I'm back on the grid with the answers they're looking for, the happier they're gonna be." Pascal shrugged. "And, forgive me if I'm wrong, of course." He nodded at Fortuna. "But I definitely have the impression we're all wearing out our welcome with our host a little."

"Not at all," Fortuna insisted, though his tone indicated otherwise. "I am... a little unused to such company these days, it seems."

"Guess that's what happens when you move to a private island," Jess said a little flippantly. "A few of Daddy's friends did it, when they got seriously rich. They all ended up becoming a bit reclusive and..." she trailed off, though Pascal was sure she had chosen her words deliberately.

"A bit what?" Fortuna said aggressively.

"Unaccustomed to socializing!" She smiled at him. "You've been everything gracious, Mr Fortuna, but you hardly know us. You're obviously only really comfortable with the people you know best."

Fortuna went very quiet after that, letting the conversation flow on without him, and Pascal could almost see the man rethinking his choices. Fortuna - when he was Sebastian Maroney, decorated CIA agent - would have had the exact same training as Pascal. The same skills. Taught to be a chameleon, to blend in, to be unnoticed, to be the pleasantly forgettable stranger an untrained person wouldn't even remember meeting if asked a few days later, never mind weeks or months.

Fortuna had obviously secretly chafed at being that person, had allowed his most flamboyant and obnoxious instincts free rein once he was no longer constrained by the Agency or indeed any sort of law-abiding principles, but had he forgotten everything he'd been taught, if he couldn't even make himself socialize with big-spending clients for a few days without losing his temper?

"We'll hold the last auction tonight," Fortuna said abruptly, a little while later. "After dinner. The winner won't be able to leave until tomorrow, unfortunately, as I can't call the helicopter back until then."

"Fine by me," Breukel said cheerfully, squeezing the waist of the girl sitting in his lap. "I'm sure Luisa can make my last evening memorable."

Breukel seemed too cheerful, for a man who'd placed last in every auction thus far. Maybe he'd just written the whole thing off at this point. Or perhaps he'd been acting all along, nudging Fortuna for information when the rest of them weren't around, trying to figure out what the high bid would need to be at the last auction, when he planned to jump in and win it at the last moment.

Pascal just wanted it all to be over, and he was sure Jess felt the same. He saw her press her fingers to her temples, guessed she was battling the same kind of stress headache he was currently managing. Much longer on Isla Fortuna and they'd probably both have stress ulcers too; it was definitely for the best they'd be leaving soon.

Fortuna didn't bother sending the girls out after dinner, just called Josef in while they were all still eating dessert and told him to bring the tablets.

Pascal once again carefully entered his bid and waited. Fortuna glanced at him once, nodded.

“Straightforward,” Fortuna murmured. “You don’t want to maybe top it up with a little of your own cash, see if you can’t get the buyer to up the ante? Or find a different buyer?”

“I’m afraid not,” Pascal replied. “I made an exclusive arrangement with the buyer, and this is their top bid. It’s not someone I’d care to cross if they discovered I’d double-crossed them. They won’t be pleased if they miss out, but they set the budget and were clear about the hard limit. There won’t be consequences to me for their decisions.”

“I think I like your buyers. You must tell me some more about them.”

Pascal just smiled. “Then they’d be your buyers, wouldn’t they? I think not.”

Fortuna chuckled and tipped his head to acknowledge the point, just as the last chime sounded. “Congratulations, General Dzhokhorov. You’ve bought yourself a nuke.”

Dzhokhorov laughed delightedly, slapping the leg of Soraya, sitting next to him. She twitched and gave him a look of dislike, which he fortunately missed.

"Come to my office," Fortuna invited, "and we will commence the transfer process. Mr Montalban, Mr Breukel… we'll talk a little later, if you don't mind. Please, stay here, enjoy my hospitality, I'll be with you once the general and I are done."

"Of course," Pascal said amiably, watching Breukel from the corner of his eye, but the other arms dealer just nodded, his attention apparently entirely focused on Luisa in his lap.

Fortuna and Dzhokharov left the room, and Pascal reached out to take Jess's hand in his, when he realized she was staring at the table. At the tablet lying in front of him, which Josef this time hadn't collected before following in Fortuna's wake.

"No," Pascal said, very quietly. He understood the temptation; it must be like laying a feast in front of a starving man and telling him to restrain himself, but taking the risk this late in the game would be foolish.

Jess's shoulders heaved as she sighed, and then she looked up at him and smiled. "It's just…" she trailed off.

“I know. But don’t.” He squeezed her hand. “We’ve done what we came to do.” At least, he hoped they had.

“Yes, I don’t suppose there’s anything useful I could do now anyway.” She spared one more wistful glance at the tablet before resolutely turning her head away.

A door banged open behind them, and Pascal turned quickly to look, seeing one of the guards coming into the room.

“Where is Mr Fortuna?” the guard barked.

“He went that way.” Jess pointed to the door on the other side of the room, and the guard ran across to it, wrenching it open without knocking.

“What’s going on?” Breukel set Luisa aside and rose to his feet, but nobody left in the dining room had any answer for him.

It was only seconds before Fortuna came striding back out with the guard on his heels, however. Breukel repeated his question but Fortuna ignored him, heading back out into the foyer area.

"Fuck it, I'm gonna follow him," Pascal said. "I don't like not knowing what's going on."

Breukel nodded, and Jess trailed along behind them. Pascal had thought the other girls would probably stay put, though as he glanced back, Soraya was following along behind Jess, a curious look on her face.

Fortuna and the guard had gone into the room off to the side of the foyer where Pascal had been the first night, the one with the window that overlooked the side alley towards the server room. A television had been switched on, tuned to a major satellite news station, and Fortuna was standing in front of it, glaring with his fists clenched at his sides.

MAJOR HOMELAND SECURITY OPERATION HITS CHURCH FACILITY, the chyron read, and Pascal felt himself tense.

"A church?" he said aloud. "Not... *Hayworth's* church?"

"Yes," Fortuna gritted out angrily.

"Wasn't his weapon supposed to be delivered tonight?"

A phone rang, startling him. Fortuna fished the device from his pocket and held it to his ear.

"Yes?" he snapped, listened for a moment. "Yes, you fucking idiot, I can see that, it's splashed all over the news! Where's the device?"

The news must have been bad, because his face darkened even further. "Where are you?" he asked finally. "Right. Go to ground. And if they somehow find you... you know what will happen to you if my name ever passes your lips." He hung up and returned his attention to the screen.

There wasn't a lot to see: the footage was clearly being shot with a long-ranged lens, as close as the cameraman in question could get to the action. Several large armored vans were drawn up at the side of a country road, but the land fell away to one side and a big ranch-type house was easily visible, several other large buildings beyond it looking more like dormitories than the horse barns other similar properties might be expected to have. What looked like about two hundred agents surrounded it, most in fairly relaxed poses with their guns away or pointed at the ground, which told Pascal whatever action there had been was long since over.

"A major operation has been conducted this evening," the news announcer was saying, "and this reporter a few minutes ago witnessed Joshua Hayworth himself being brought out in handcuffs and loaded into a vehicle for transport. No statement has yet been forthcoming from any of the agents on the scene."

The footage changed for a moment to show a long-range shot of a white-haired man being put into an armored car. Two other men in cuffs followed, each surrounded by agents. And even at the camera's long range, the last man was clearly Saul Hayworth.

"*Fuck,*" Fortuna snarled. "That fucking idiot. No idea of operational security."

Fortuna was assuming the leak had to be on Hayworth's end. Pascal exhaled silently, but didn't dare glance at Jess.

The camera returned to what Pascal figured was live footage, focusing on the agents milling around the armored vans, all wearing tactical clothing and most of them with dark blue windbreakers over the top with HOMELAND SECURITY on their backs.

The closest agent to the camera turned and pointed in the camera's direction, saying something to one of their colleagues. It was a woman, Pascal saw as the camera zoomed in on her face. A pretty woman with hair a not-quite-natural shade of dark red...

Jess went totally rigid beside him just as Pascal recognized her sister.

What's Liane doing there?

She looked too much like Jess. She looked *exactly* like Jess, barring the different hair color, and Pascal knew the instant Fortuna saw the resemblance, because the breath hissed between his teeth an instant before he spun around.

There was no bluffing it out. Jess's expression told the whole story in an instant, and Fortuna yelled in wordless fury even as his hand swooped for the small of his back and the gun he was wearing under his shirt there.

Fast as Fortuna was, Pascal was even quicker. He dived for the only other weapon in the room, the gun in the hip holster of the guard, who hadn't the faintest idea what was going on and no suspicion he was about to be jumped.

"Run!" he roared at Jess, praying she wouldn't freeze, and sent up a silent prayer of thanks that she didn't, whirling on her heel and gone before Fortuna could even get his hand to his gun.

He had no time to worry about her, because Fortuna had his gun out now, and Pascal couldn't get the guard's gun out of his holster, only had time to jerk the man in front of him as a human shield... and Fortuna's first double tap hit his own man right in the chest.

Breukel was yelling with shock, backing towards the door with his hands up in the air. It seemed that Fortuna could no longer distinguish between friend or foe, though, because he shot Breukel twice between the eyes before spinning back towards Pascal.

Pascal had the guard's gun in hand now, though he kept the limp body held up as a kind of shield. He lifted the gun, snapping the safety off and pulling the trigger twice.

Fortuna grinned. "Ouch," he said mildly.

Fuck! Blanks!

Fortuna didn't even trust his own men.

"I'm going to cut her into little tiny pieces," Fortuna said, his tone almost conversational.

If he was going to waste time talking, Pascal wasn't about to look a gift horse in the mouth. A few precious seconds where Fortuna wasn't shooting him in the head would do nicely.

He threw himself backwards out of the window.

Chapter 22

Jess ran as fast as she could, past a shocked-looking Soraya, back into the dining-room and through into the office beyond, where she met Josef coming the other way, obviously having heard the shots, gun already in his hand.

"It's Breukel!" she cried, thinking fast. "He shot Mr Fortuna..."

"Out of the way," Josef growled, sweeping out his arm to shove her to one side, and she stabbed the steak knife she'd stolen dinner on the first night and had been carrying around ever since straight into his left eye with all her strength.

Josef never even made a sound, just collapsed in a heap. Jess had his gun in hand before he'd even hit the ground, spun around and charged back in the other direction. There was a tremendous smashing sound, another shot rang out, and by the time she got back to the lounge room, both Pascal and Fortuna were gone and there was only the breeze blowing in through the shattered window and two dead bodies on the floor.

"What's going on?" Soraya shouted and clutched at her arm.

Jess shook her off. "Get the other girls and hide, if you want to live," she said succinctly.

Soraya took one look at her face, grabbed Luisa, who was peeking out of the dining room, and gabbled at her in rapid Spanish. The other three girls had already taken shelter under the furniture, but Soraya called to them, obviously telling them to come out, and they all started for the door to the kitchens, probably thinking to get the other staff.

Dzhokharov, Jess thought. Pascal could take care of himself, and he and Fortuna were obviously battling it out. She winced as she heard another distant gunshot, instincts clamoring at her to go after Pascal and try to help. But Jess couldn't leave the Chechen at their backs. She looked down at the gun in her hand. A stubby Sig Sauer P320; she'd never handled one before but recognized it, knew how to handle it. She flicked the manual safety lever and rested her finger on the trigger guard, cautiously approaching the door to Fortuna's office.

The office was empty, and a door on the other side stood open. Dzhokharov was gone.

"Shit," Jess said under her breath, eyeing the laptop computer open on the desk. Running a quick mental calculation.

No. If it all goes wrong here, they'll need to know it's kicked off. Time to call in the cavalry.

She crouched down behind the desk and pulled the laptop down to the floor, laying the gun right beside it. If anyone looked in either door, they might not see her immediately. And hopefully, she'd only need a couple of minutes.

Jess couldn't believe her eyes when she looked at the screen. Dzhokharov had left it open on a crypto wallet app. Logged in.

Do I have the time?

I'll make the time.

Her fingers danced over the keyboard, alerting her own people that things were kicking off on Isla Fortuna - they'd already know exactly where it was from her original hack - and it was time to send in whatever cavalry they had available. One of the target devices is still here as of this moment, she added, and then flipped back to the crypto wallet. With a grin, she set about rapidly ensuring Dzhokhorov wouldn't have the funding to purchase so much as an airline ticket back to Chechnya.

She could hear distant shouting, but surprisingly not many gunshots. She and Pascal had counted ten guards and two other assistants on Josef's level who were all armed, apart from Fortuna himself. Considering the chaos she and Pascal had just kicked off, she'd have expected a lot more shooting to be going on.

Closing the laptop and tucking it under her arm, Jess darted quietly to the door Dzhokharov must have used, finding that it led outside, an exit on the side of the main resort building. She listened, heard Fortuna yelling orders, someone swearing back at him in Spanish. Frowned.

Did that guy say what I think he said? Did he just accuse Fortuna of giving them dud guns?

She looked down at the gun in her own hand. It was Josef's, and Fortuna had obviously trusted Josef with quite a lot. Was Fortuna really paranoid enough to give his own people dummy bullets?

It was the work of a moment to eject the magazine and look at the round visible on the top. It looked like a proper round to Jess, but surely, the other guards would have noticed before now if the bullets they'd been given looked like blanks? She slid the round out, weighed it in her hand. It felt no different to any other real round she'd ever handled, and while she'd never been a field agent, she'd still had to achieve and maintain a decent standard when she worked for the NSA.

Guess there's only one way to find out.

She'd already decided what she was going to do. She'd deal with Fortuna if she came across him, but her plan was to find Mariska and make sure she was safe, protect her until whatever US forces were coming arrived to secure the place.

All the lights on the island went out as Jess was running down the path to the girls' dormitory, and she stumbled briefly before recovering her footing. *Pascal*, she thought with a small grin. No way would Fortuna have turned his own lights off. Pascal was still alive and out there causing chaos.

The door to the dormitory was open and the place appeared empty when she got there. Jess risked cracking the laptop open for a few seconds, long enough for the screen to come to life and give her a little light to see.

"Mariska?" she hissed. "Are you here? It's Jess! I've come to help."

Something cold touched the side of her neck. "And just what do you think you can help with?"

It was a woman's voice. Accented. Spanish. Jess didn't move her head.

"Can't you hear the gunshots? I wanted to get Mariska so we can hide," she said.

"That's why you have a gun, is it? And a computer? Where the hell did you get that?"

Whatever she's got against my neck, it's not a gun. Jess took a calculated risk, leapt forward quickly and wheeled around, bringing the gun up.

"Camila?" she said, startled.

In the faint light from the laptop screen, the other girl looked very different. Hair pulled back in a no-nonsense ponytail, she looked calm and resolute. And while it wasn't a gun in her hand, the heavy, serrated-blade bread knife could do some serious damage... and if that was really blood dripping off the blade, it already had.

Camila just looked at her for a moment, and then she lowered her knife. "CIA?" she asked.

Oh my God. She's an undercover agent too.

"Homeland Security," Jess said. It was close enough to the truth, and it would take too long to explain otherwise.

"Guàlizean Secret Police," Camila said, causing Jess's jaw to drop. "I already hid Mariska. Come with me. Does that laptop still have internet connection, with the power out?"

"Probably not, but let's get somewhere concealed and have a look." Still stunned, Jess followed Camila, who led her around behind the dormitory and into a stand of palm trees, then scrambled over some rocks. It was tough going with the laptop and the gun, but Jess certainly wasn't going to put anything down. Camila finally stopped after clambering through some bushes, and Jess followed her into a small clearing beyond. One where Camila had clearly been quite busy setting up a little escape nest of sorts... where Mariska was sitting on a blanket, face pale in the moonlight.

"Jess!" Mariska burst out, trying to get to her feet.

"Sh, stay there." Jess crouched, put the laptop down briefly to give Mariska a quick hug. "You okay?"

"Yes. What's happening? Is Mr Montalban..."

"He's the one who turned the lights out." *I hope.* "He'll come looking for us. Help is on the way." *It better be...*

"Can I see the laptop?" Camila asked, and Jess nodded, handing it over.

"Why is the Guàlizean Secret Police here?" she asked quietly, watching as Camila tapped at the keyboard. "Isn't this Venezuelan territory?"

"Technically, but he's got fingers in too many pies in Guàlize City. We've been watching him for months, but couldn't get anyone in until I volunteered to go to Caracas and get in with the crew of high-end sex workers he brings in occasionally. I've been on and off this island three times, but I've never been able to get access to any of his computers until now." Camila made a face, closing the lid of the laptop. "Internet connection is down, with the power out. I need to take this with me."

"Uh, no, I'm taking it with *me*," Jess said firmly.

"You already hacked the place. Leave me a crumb, at least." Camila's teeth were white in the moonlight as she grinned. "I saw you, that second night. I was going to try and break into that server room myself. You were already in there."

Jess couldn't believe it. She mentally kicked herself; she'd made the exact same mistake she had counted on Fortuna and the others making with her. She'd dismissed the other girls on the island as unimportant players in the game without really thinking about them. Camila had undoubtedly played up the beating she'd received from Hayworth, maybe even incited him to violence, so that she'd be left alone and ignored, giving her free rein to sneak about and get up to mischief.

She opened her mouth to say something, but Mariska grabbed at her arm.

"Sh! Someone coming!" the Chechen girl whispered, eyes wide with panic.

The three of them stayed very still and quiet. Male voices sounded close by.

"Bring me the Chechen girl." It was Fortuna's voice. "Montalban's woman will come for her. I could see it; she was soft-hearted over the kid."

"Yes, boss." A flashlight flickered; someone was going into the women's dormitory. "Nobody here, boss," the guard called back a moment later, and Fortuna swore.

"Find them! They can't have got far. The girl was hurt, could barely walk. Unless Dzhokharov came for her." He seemed almost to be musing to himself aloud. "Where is that bastard, anyway? I can't believe he would be working with the Americans."

The guard was waiting patiently for further instructions; Fortuna turned on him suddenly, waving his gun. "Why are you standing around? Find that fucking girl and bring her to me!"

"Where will you be, boss?" the guard asked, tone almost placid. He seemed quite accustomed to Fortuna's sudden rages. Obviously the ex-IA renegade didn't bother to rein in his temper around his staff.

"The safe, where I have the device." Fortuna seemed to calm. "That's my leverage. Montalban will want to secure it. Fuck, Dzhokharov will be trying to get it too. They'll come to me. Bring me the girl, and find the others."

"Yes, boss."

Footsteps sounded, moving away, but the flashlight stayed steady. The guard began to move around, shining the light into the bushes, muttering to himself. "Girl! You hiding?" he called out. "You can come out now, no more trouble!"

Camila touched Jess's wrist lightly. When Jess looked at her, the Guàlizean agent gestured towards the gun in Jess's hand, but then shook her head and put her finger to her lips.

Don't use the gun, too loud, Jess mentally interpreted, and nodded. Camila held up her knife and pointed to herself, then towards the guard's bobbing flashlight.

Oh my God. Camila was so matter-of fact about it! Yes, Jess had killed Josef, but that had been in the heat of the moment and she knew she was going to be doing some serious soul-searching about it later.

Camila didn't even wait for Jess to respond; not that Jess even had the slightest idea what to do, apart from trying to discourage her. Camila just slipped quietly out of their sheltered little hollow and was gone into the night.

Sixty seconds later, there was a muffled, abruptly cut-off cry, and then the sound of something heavy hitting the ground.

"She kill him too?" Mariska whispered, and Jess decided she was definitely not going to ask how many men Camila had killed before Jess found them.

"Yes," she answered quietly, as Camila stepped into view below them and beckoned. "I have to go, Mariska, but I think you should stay here, where it's safe. Help is coming; don't come out until the island is secured. If... if something happens and you can't find me? Remember this name and keep saying it until someone listens to you. Liane Hagerty, Hestia Global Security. You got that?"

"I got it. But I am coming with you." Mariska pushed herself to her feet with a little wince of pain, but she was clearly determined. "I will carry that. You and Camila both think it's important. I look after it for you." She pointed at the laptop, and Jess hesitated only a moment before handing it over.

“It’s not more important than you are. If you have to use it to stop a bullet, don’t hesitate.” She tried to keep her tone light and teasing. Saw Mariska’s tense shoulders relax minutely as she took the laptop and wrapped her arms around it tightly.

“That gun might be no good,” Jess said in a soft undertone as they rejoined Camila, who was rifling through the fallen guard’s pockets. “I think Fortuna didn’t trust his guards. One of them was yelling about his bullets being blanks.”

Camila said several swear words in Spanish, but she also picked up the bloody break knife she’d discarded by the guard’s body and kept it in her left hand as they moved quietly back towards the main resort building.

Jess found herself wishing she’d pulled the knife back out of Josef, now, but she guessed in a pinch the Sig Sauer would make a pretty effective bludgeon, if her bullets turned out to be blanks after all.

Fire lit up the night ahead of them, and Jess swore and pushed Mariska into the shadows of the building they were passing. Someone had set fire to the thatched roof of a decorative gazebo - one of Fortuna's people, trying to make a bit of light to see by? She guessed it wasn't Pascal. He was the one who'd turned out the lights, for sure. No way would he give up the advantage of the darkness.

"Whoever that is," she whispered to Camila, "it has to be the enemy. It won't be Pascal."

"Then let's take care of them."

They'd only taken one step forward, though, when there was an absolutely deafening boom, an explosion going off at the top of the island.

"Fuck me!" Jess threw herself flat by instinct, before hastily crawling backwards to rejoin the others.

"Did Pascal do that?" Mariska said, awed, as they watched flames shooting up into the night sky, dwarfing the smaller fire close to them. "That's Fortuna's villa, no?"

"Yes." Camila grinned viciously. "Oh, he won't like that."

That was Pascal's work, for sure. He was still alive and out there looking to cause chaos, and that explosion was going to draw everyone like a magnet. Which meant, if Jess understood anything about Pascal's tactics at all, that he'd be behind them, waiting to ambush them as they ran blindly into the chaos.

She was more than willing to help, but she also needed to find him and tell him she'd summoned help. It couldn't be that far away now, surely… CIA would have pre-positioned Navy ships close enough to send help in fast.

Or at least, she hoped so.

"Come on. I need to find Pascal." She began to move forward again, Camila and Mariska following her, but the enormous chatter of automatic gunfire up ahead, muzzle flashes lighting up the dark further, made them all drop to the ground again. A second later, though, Jess realized they weren't in danger; the gunfire was aimed in a different direction entirely. "Fortuna's broken out the heavy artillery!" That was no semi-automatic, no AR-15 or UZI. That was a fully automatic, military grade machine gun.

"He *is* an arms dealer!" Camila yelled at her over the deafening noise, before it abruptly cut off.

Fair point. And if he was shooting at Pascal, then her partner was in deep shit. Jess took a deep breath.

"Stay with Mariska," she told Camila. "I'm going to try and take out whoever has that gun from behind."

"You're fucking nuts!" Camila said, but she took Mariska's arm and started to back up.

"Go hide. I'll find you!" Jess cast Mariska one brief look, one she hoped was reassuring, before she began to run.

Chapter 23

The absolute best thing he could do for Jess was keep Fortuna busy, so the second Pascal hit the ground in a hail of glass, he leaped back up and ran like hell. Fortuna fired another shot out the window, roaring with rage, and Pascal heard the crunch of his shoes in the glass as the arms dealer followed him out.

"What's the matter, Maroney?" Pascal yelled back as he ran around the first corner he came from.

"*What* did you call me?" Fortuna sounded genuinely astonished, and he'd stopped moving. Pascal couldn't hear his stupid Loubisharks squeaking any more.

"Sebastian Maroney? You didn't really think the CIA had entirely lost track of you, did you? Deputy Director Spires would very much like a word." Pascal was taking a shot in the dark with that one, but Spires was right about the same age as Fortuna. The odds that they would have known each other were pretty good.

"That fucking stupid bitch! How she ever made Deputy Director is beyond me." A slight squeak. Fortuna was moving again. Pascal waited, right at the corner, prepared to grab at Fortuna when he rounded it. He'd bet on himself in a grapple against the other man. Fortuna had gotten lazy and Pascal very much doubted he was keeping up any kind of exercise routine.

Except he didn't come around the corner: there was the click of a door closing instead, and Pascal swore under his breath. Fortuna had started thinking again, wasn't going to walk into an ambush. Was probably going to use his superior knowledge of the island's buildings and terrain to get around behind Pascal and try to ambush him...

He whirled and ran.

Jess was smart enough to find somewhere to hide, he figured, but he needed to keep Fortuna off balance, keep him from regrouping. He needed a working weapon, but the only one he knew for sure had real bullets was Fortuna's own.

And there would probably be more in Fortuna's own private villa, the one at the top of the hill, the one nobody else was allowed in. Pascal needed to get up there pronto and find himself an equalizer.

But first, he needed a distraction, and he needed to make it much harder for Fortuna and his guards to move around with impunity, so he ran for a critical piece of infrastructure he'd noted on the very first day. It was the work of a few seconds to grab a rock from the ground and smash the lock on the power box, a few more to flip switches and start ripping fuses and wires out, doing as much damage as he could with his bare hands and a rock. Sparks flew and every light on the island went out in an instant. Shouts went up, and Pascal grinned.

That'll keep them busy.

The dark was his friend. He ran silently up the hill, listening to the shouts above him, stepping off the path into the darker shadows beneath some palms when two guards came blundering down past him, calling to their fellows, asking what was wrong.

Fortuna didn't even invest in radios for them. Lazy, overconfident... Pascal could hardly believe a former CIA agent could have fallen so far. He kept running, jumped over the five-foot fence surrounding the private villa, and didn't even bother looking for a door, just kicked in a window and went in that way. If a guard heard him and came looking, he was about to get a nasty surprise.

The villa was luxurious, but it was only four rooms. It took Pascal just seconds to search it and find a locked door, and seconds more to rip the leg off a chair and use it to crowbar his way in.

Light. He needed a damn light. Hamstrung by his own cleverness. He found candles and a cigarette lighter in a drawer in the kitchenette - a hurricane emergency kit. Adequate for what he needed right now. He didn't light anything just yet, pausing to check quickly outside, shaking his head at the incompetence of the guards who'd abandoned their posts at the first signs of trouble. No wonder Fortuna hadn't trusted them with real bullets.

The brief flame that sparked from the lighter had Pascal's jaw dropping with what he saw inside that closet. "My, my," he murmured, before he lit a candle, set it in the doorway carefully - well away from what was inside the closet - and started grabbing.

He was sorely tempted by a futuristic-looking machine gun, what he was pretty sure was a Sig Sauer XM250, the one the US Army had recently contracted to purchase but wouldn't even start to be delivered for another year at least, but instead grabbed for a more familiar FN-SCAR, though he thought it was the newer SCAR-H model rather than the SCAR-L he'd used in his time in the Rangers. The four matching 20-round magazines were empty, and he cursed softly under his breath and grabbed a box of the 7.62mm rounds from a low shelf, filling one mag as fast as he could manage. He'd try and fill the others on the run. Several grenades for his pockets completed the haul he'd need - now to make sure nobody else would be arming up in here. He grabbed a red canister with a grin.

"That'll do nicely!" He primed the incendiary grenade as he ran, turned and threw it back inside the closet door just before diving back out through the window he'd entered in and covering his ears as he crouched low to the ground.

The explosion knocked him flat, but only for a moment, and then he was up and running, shoving rounds into another magazine as he went, vaulting over the fence and diving into the undergrowth on the other side.

A scream of what sounded like absolutely primal rage came from below him. Fortuna, Pascal guessed, losing his shit completely at Pascal's sabotage. Hopefully, that was Fortuna's only backup arsenal.

A second later, that hope was dashed completely as bullets started tearing through the trees. Pascal flung himself flat again, cursing luridly. That was another machine gun, and he had no doubt it was Fortuna wielding it, crazed with rage and determined to destroy him.

I've got to get off this hill. He knows I have to be up here. He slung his rifle around to his back and belly-crawled down through the undergrowth as fast as he could go. A woman's scream somewhere ahead made his hiss under his breath and go even faster.

"Oh, shit." Jess paused in her scramble through the trees, turned to look behind her. She was pretty sure that was Mariska. A moment later, Dzhokharov came into view, silhouetted against the background of the burning gazebo; he was dragging Mariska by her hair.

"Get down here, you fucking bitch!" That was Fortuna shouting, though she couldn't see him. "Give yourself up, or Ruslan will gut her!"

She's his wife. Would he…? Yes, he would. Mariska was whimpering and crying, and though Jess probably had a shot on

Dzhokharov, she couldn't see Fortuna, and she didn't even know if the bullets in her gun were real.

"You've got until I count to ten. One. Two."

"I'm coming!" she shouted, hoping to get him to stop or at least slow the count. Buy a little time. *Where are you, Pascal?*

"Don't you fucking dare," Pascal's voice said, shockingly close, and she whirled around.

"Pascal?" she hissed it, trying not to alert anyone else to their whereabouts.

"THREE!" Fortuna roared. "FOUR!"

A shrub rustled in front of her, and Pascal stood up. "Don't go out there, Jess!"

"I have to, he'll kill her!"

"He'll kill you both if you do!"

"SEVEN!"

"I'm sorry..." she dropped her gun, turned, and ran. Trusting Pascal to pick it up and make the shot when he got the opportunity.

If those bullets are real...

She pushed the thought away and ran faster.

"TEN!"

"I'm here!" She skidded to a stop just a few feet from Dzhokharov, her hands held up to show she was unarmed. "Let her go. You don't want to hurt her. She's your *wife*."

"Useless bitch can't even breed me a son." Dzhokharov flung Mariska to the ground. "Maybe I take you back to Chechnya instead, American spy. Chain you to bed and breed you until I put a son in your belly. Cut it out and do it all over again. Make you useful."

Jess tried not to recoil in instant revulsion. "You're not man enough," she said scornfully. "Us girls talk, you know. I know what you've got." She curled her little finger deliberately.

Dzhokhorov's face twisted with rage, and he stepped forward, reaching for her. Even as she stepped back to evade, Jess caught movement behind him. The flash of silver reflecting flames as Mariska lifted Camila's bloody bread knife and rose from the ground, stabbing it with every bit of strength in her small body into her husband's back.

"Run!" Jess screamed, not waiting for Dzhokhorov to fall, nor for Fortuna to realize what had just happened. She grabbed Mariska's hand, dragging it away from the knife blade, and they ran for their lives.

Gunfire rattled behind them, not the terrible clatter of the machine gun, but three-round bursts, precise - covering fire. *Pascal*, Jess realized. He'd somehow gotten hold of an assault rifle and was covering their escape, though at the cost of revealing his own position. The machine gun roared in response.

"Where's Camila?" Jess hissed as she and Mariska fled.

"Ruslan hit her head and she fell down," Mariska gasped back. "She kill another guard who found us, but he came up behind us and hit her."

"She might still be alive. We need to find her..."

A sudden roar of sound made them both look up, moments before powerful searchlights swept across them.

"Helicopters," Mariska whispered.

“Help,” Jess said succinctly. “Let’s find Camila and hide you. I need to go find Pascal.”

“You go. I can do this.” Mariska stood tall. “I kill Ruslan. I kill anyone else who try to stop me, too.”

Jess hated to leave her, but the machine gun fire hadn’t stopped. Fortuna had just changed targets, firing up at the helicopters, which were being forced to retreat. Jess doubted it would be long before the island was swarming with friendlies, though.

“Just be careful who you kill,” she said to Mariska before letting go of her hand and whirling around to run back into the fight again.

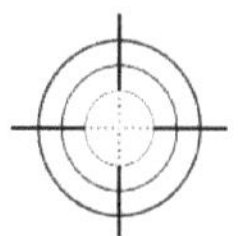

Fortuna had lost his mind, and Pascal had to stop him, now, before he managed to shoot down one of those helicopters. He ran down the hill, heedless of the blood flowing from a gash on his ribs where a bullet had gouged a thick furrow along his side. He'd been unbelievably lucky it hadn't gone straight through him, but he counted it a small price to pay for the precious few seconds he'd bought for Jess and Mariska to flee. He'd made sure to put at least a couple of shots into Dzhokhorov; the Chechen had fallen to his knees, but was still alive and trying to reach around behind him to pull out the knife. After Pascal's shots, the general went face down and stopped moving.

"Good fucking riddance," Pascal muttered as he sprinted past Dzhokhorov's body, pulling a grenade from his pocket and priming it, keeping his thumb on the pressure plate until he reached throwing range of Fortuna's position, impossible to miss as the arms dealer kept shooting at the helicopters. "Hey, asshole," he yelled. "The CIA says hello!"

Fortuna spun back towards him, mouth opening, but the grenade had already left Pascal's hand, the fuze already halfway through its three-second timer. Fortuna didn't even have time to let out a scream before the grenade exploded in mid-air, less than three feet from his face.

Pascal had flung himself flat yet again, knowing the explosion was coming. The shock wave still crushed him for a moment, his ears ringing as the world went briefly very white and very loud.

“Pascal. Pascal!”

Someone was shouting his name. Dazed, he blinked up at Jess as she grabbed at his arm, rolling him over onto his back. Pulling the SCAR from his hands and looking around, crouching over his prone form. She looked competent and deadly and he let himself just lie there for a moment, admiring her.

“You’d better let me have that,” he tried to say, but the words came out weirdly slurred and garbled, and he frowned.

Pascal’s voice didn’t sound right, and Jess paused in scanning the area for threats to look down at him.

"You're hurt," she said, and it wasn't a question. There was blood as well as dirt on his face.

"S'a graze," he slurred, feeling at his side, and she saw to her horror blood on his shirt as well. His eyes drifted shut.

"Pascal, don't you dare! Stay with me! Open your eyes!"

She could hear shouting now. Voices calling her real name, and Pascal's.

"Help's here. I called them in, everything's going to be fine. Pascal? Open your eyes!" She took one hand off the gun to feel for his pulse, his throat slippery with blood as she fumbled at his frantically. "Don't you dare die on me now. Not after everything!"

She was still shouting at him when strong hands took the gun from her unresisting hands, lifted her away from his body.

"We've got him, Miss Hagerty. Let us take him."

"Pascal," she sobbed, finally breaking down, the tears running down her face.

“We’ve got him.”

It was an American voice, and she blinked back the tears fiercely, looking up at the absolutely massive soldier in front of her. He wasn’t wearing an American uniform; she tried to make her eyes focus on the flag stitched on the breast of his jungle fatigues.

“Who are you?” she mumbled, swaying like a leaf in the breeze.

“Jack MacAuley. Former Army Ranger, now with the Guàlizean Secret Police. We were put on standby by Deputy Director Spires two days ago as the closest rapid reaction force to this location. There are more reinforcements on the way, but we got here first.”

“Oh. Guàlizean. I met one of your people. Camila? I don’t know her last name.”

She sounded slow and stupid, and Jess recognized vaguely that she might be going into shock. MacAuley peered in her eyes, grasped her forearm and gave her a gentle shake.

“Steady, Miss Hagerty. I need you to show me where the device is. I need to secure it, do you understand? I work for the Guàlizeans but that device needs to be in US hands."

She nodded, understanding what he meant. Looked at Pascal, now being worked on by two combat medics.

"I'm sorry, but you have to leave him. Let them take care of him." MacAuley pulled on her arm. "The device?"

"In the main building. The old hotel safe." She took a deep breath, made herself look away from Pascal. She couldn't do any more for him than they could. "This way."

The safe was locked, and Jess suspected the keys were likely in Fortuna's pocket and very possibly blown to bits along with him. She told MacAuley as much, and the big soldier just looked grave and planted himself in front of the safe door.

"Then I'll be waiting here until Deputy Director Spires gives me leave to go. And I think you'd better stay too. Looks like Montoya's not in any shape to tell us what we need to know, so why don't you start filling me in while we wait."

Jess's legs wouldn't quite hold her up. She slid to the floor in a graceless heap, ended up sitting with her back against the wall.

"You doin' okay there, Miss Hagerty? Do I need the medics for you too?" MacAuley asked.

"No, I'm not injured. Just... tired. Really tired."

"Stay awake and talk to me," he ordered. "How many other hostiles are on the island?"

She half-laughed. "Still alive? No idea. Camila took out I don't know how many with her bread knife, and Pascal must have killed a few, and I stabbed Josef through the eye..."

"I think you'd better start at the beginning," MacAuley said after a moment of slightly stunned silence.

Jess talked for what felt like hours. Helicopters came and went above, several of them; MacAuley told her at one point that Pascal had been airlifted to Guàlize City for medical treatment.

"He'll be alright. The wound on his side is worse than he probably thought it was; he's lost a fair bit of blood but my wife will patch him up."

"Your wife?" Jess blinked wearily up at the big agent.

"She's on the trauma response team at the Santa Maria hospital." MacAuley grinned, obviously proud of his spouse. "Don't worry about Montoya." He paused a moment, obviously listening to information coming through on his tactical radio. "My people have found Camila too. She's alive; concussed from the looks of things. They'll get her on the next chopper out."

"What about Mariska?" Jess mumbled.

"And who's she?"

"A young Chechen girl. She was here with one of the buyers, General Dzhokhorov, but she's just a kid."

"Any uninjured non-hostiles will be held for debriefing," MacAuley said, not unkindly. "Likely enough your people will end up with her, since she's not a local. It's still all to be worked out exactly whose jurisdiction this all is, but to avoid an incident with our

Venezuelan neighbors, highly likely Guàlize will blame it all on the US and pretend we were never here."

"Plausibly deniable?"

"Something like that." MacAuley tipped his head. Murmured something into his radio. "Sounds like your boss is here?"

"My boss?" Jess's brow furrowed. She didn't have the energy to get off the floor when Deputy Director Spires came striding in, surrounded by black-clad, heavily armed agents, and stood looking down at her. "Oh. Hi." She waggled her fingers, about all that she could summon up the energy to do.

Spires' hard face softened minutely at the sight of her. "Miss Hagerty. Looks like you've had a busy evening."

"Mm hm. It's in there. Or it was." Jess waved her hand vaguely at the safe door.

Spires jerked her head to one of the men with her, who stepped forward to have a low-voiced conversation with MacAuley. Spires herself squatted down to put herself on an eye level with Jess.

"Well done, Miss Hagerty," she said quietly. "Very well done. I had my doubts you could pull it off, but the data hack you pulled off was absolute gold. We've tracked down all sorts of equipment that was already in, or was destined for, the wrong hands. You've saved countless lives."

"Oh," Jess said, a little stunned. "And you have both the other devices? We saw the raid on the Hayworth compound on the news..."

"Yep, your sister inserted herself on the raid. That device is secured and the entire leadership of the church is likely to be in prison for a very, very long time. The Korean device isn't in our hands yet, but we know where it is and the Navy should have it safe within the next few hours."

"Good." Jess had already decided she wasn't going to tell anyone that it had been the sight of Liane on the television which had triggered the crisis. It might get back to her sister, and Jess wouldn't have that knowledge on Liane's consciousness. "Hey. I need a favor."

Spires grinned. "I think you've earned a few. What is it?"

"There's a girl. Mariska. She's Chechen. I know you'll need to debrief her, but don't lose her, okay? I have plans for her."

The edges of Jess's vision were beginning to go dark. She felt herself begin to slump sideways, no longer able to hold herself upright against the wall as the last of her strength ran out. "And tell Pascal," she mumbled, but the words didn't come out, and the last thing she saw was Spires's amused expression change to one of concern as everything went dark.

Chapter 24

Pascal pushed the button on the intercom and waited, glancing back over his shoulder at the rental car behind him, checking it was parked far enough off the road he wouldn't get sideswiped by a passing driver. He'd been to Hestia's offices first, where Liane regretfully told him Jessikah was taking a personal day… and then added with a grin that she was pretty sure Jess was at home.

The gate slid noiselessly open after a couple of minutes, long enough for Pascal to start wondering if Liane was wrong. He jumped back in the driver's seat and eased the car inside, halting it on the driveway and looking admiringly at the house. Jess really was doing very well for herself.

The massive timber-and-frosted-glass door slid silently open, and there she was - hair once again dyed that gorgeous aqua mermaid shade of blue, a loose white sundress not hiding the fact that she'd lost weight and looked a little too thin, her feet bare.

"Pascal," she said disbelievingly, almost hanging on to the door. "What..."

"I brought you a visitor," he said, gesturing, and Mariska erupted from the passenger seat of the car and flung herself at Jess.

"Oh, my God!" Jess threw her arms around Mariska, embracing her tightly as the Chechen girl started to sob into her shoulder. "*Pascal.*" Jess's own blue eyes shimmered with tears. "Come in. Both of you... come in."

Jess settled them both at her kitchen table, poured glasses of ice water. Put her hand on Mariska's shoulder, as if barely able to believe the other girl was really there. Pascal grinned at the affectionate gesture.

"Looks great, doesn't she?" he said fondly.

Mariska certainly did. A month of decent food and some therapy - after a couple of days intensive debriefing - had done wonders. Her hair looked shiny, her eyes were bright, and she wore comfortable shorts, T-shirt and sneakers; much more appropriate for a girl her age than the skimpy dresses Dzhokhorov had made her wear.

“She looks wonderful. So do you.” Jess made an abortive little gesture, half-reaching for him, but dropped her hand. “You’ve recovered okay?”

“All fine.” The bandages had finally come off only three days earlier, but he wasn’t about to tell her that. “Sorry I gave you a scare.”

“Yes, I’d call almost bleeding to death giving me a scare!” Jess gave him a severe look.

Mariska flinched, and her hand crept into Pascal’s. Jess saw, and she gave him a startled, wide-eyed look.

“I asked if I could be appointed Mariska’s legal guardian,” Pascal said quickly, heading off whatever Jess might be wondering. “There’s a lot of paperwork to be completed for her, of course, but… if I legally adopt her, the path to US citizenship becomes much smoother."

"He says I can call him Dad," Mariska said gleefully.

"Oh my God." Jess but a hand over her mouth, her eyes welling with tears again.

"I want to go to American school. Learn… things. All the things I do not know." Mariska shrugged. "It might take a while, but I will do it. Dad promised to help."

"I did." He gave her a fond smile, squeezing her hand. "And… we were talking about other things, too. I'm not going undercover anymore, for obvious reasons - I have a daughter depending on me now. And a desk job at Langley isn't quite my speed, nor do I want to be attached to some overseas embassy."

"So?" Jess asked, folding her arms. She looked as though she was hardly daring to hope.

"Well, the government is suitably grateful for what we did, of course. I can pretty much name the agency and location I'd like to be transferred to. The FBI have a large office here in LA… or you did mention there might be an opening for me at Hestia."

"I did, didn't I?" A small smile touched her lips, and she looked at Mariska. "You know, there's a really great school not far from here. Several kids of Hestia's employees go there, and come to think of it, the principal owes me a favor… I sorted out a small cyberbullying issue they were dealing with a couple of years back. If you two were living in the school district, I'm sure I could get Mariska in."

There were stars in Mariska's eyes, and she looked from Pascal to Jess and back again, desperately pleading.

"Bet the rental market around here's pretty terrible, though," Pascal said, confident now what Jess's answer would be, but unable to resist teasing Mariska just a little more.

"Dreadful. This is a big house, though. I think I could tolerate a couple of room-mates." Jess burst out laughing as Mariska shrieked with delight and leaped up to hug her.

"Oh Jess. Oh. I love you so much. And you, Dad - I love you both!"

"If you're going to call him Dad," Jess said, "you could maybe think about calling me Mom. If that wouldn't be too weird."

"Mom." Mariska tried it out, before her smile bloomed again, lighting up her pretty face. "No. No, is not weird, is *perfect*."

"I think so too." Jess kissed Mariska's forehead.

"Can we get a cat?" Mariska looked up at her beseechingly, and Jess laughed again.

"We're going to have our hands full with a demanding teenager, I see. But yes, of course we can. If that's what you think we need to make us a proper family."

Mariska adorably jumped up and down with excitement.

"Why don't you go and explore? Just don't touch any of the computers when you get to my study," Jess called after her as Mariska turned and almost ran out, as happy and excited as a much younger child on Christmas morning.

"We did just give her a new home and a family and promise her a cat," Pascal pointed out when Jess shook her head in amusement. "She's doing great, but everything is a lot for her to process right now. She'll probably have a meltdown and cry herself to sleep later."

"Good to know." Jess nodded, obviously mentally filing away the information, and if Pascal knew her at all, probably already thinking up strategies to help Mariska settle in more comfortably.

They looked at each other for a long moment in silence, and then Jess smiled, soft and tender. "So," she said, coming forward and slipping onto Pascal's lap, her arms winding around his neck. "Big jump, from undercover fake dating to working together for real and co-parenting a traumatized Chechen teenager."

"It is," he agreed. "And I wouldn't blame you if it was too much for you."

"It's not." She leaned in. Kissed him, slow and lingering. "It's not too much at all," she whispered against his mouth.

He stroked his hands down her back, savoring the feel of her in his arms. "I have a question," he murmured. "Off the record."

“Mm?”

“Mariska was clutching a laptop when she was picked up. Fortuna had fragged the servers himself, and I blew up whatever computers were in his villa, so it was all we had left physically. And there were some crypto transaction details on there that CIA couldn’t quite make sense of… stuff that somehow didn’t get copied over through your worm hack to what we were seeing on the outside. All the money the Chechen rebels had, for example. Got transferred into some other crypto accounts, then out to real-world bank accounts, then back into different crypto wallets, then back out again… and that’s where our forensic accountants lost the trail.”

“Fortuna must have set up something automated to do that,” Jess said blandly.

“Interesting, that. All the crypto wallets Fortuna had that we were able to identify - the ones Hayworth and Yoon transferred their payments into, for example - they didn’t do that. The coins were still sitting there.”

“How odd.” Jess tilted her head, her eyes innocently wide.

"Off the record, Jess."

Her smile widened. "Well, if we are *really* talking off the record. Mariska deserves some nice things in her life. Twenty million dollars should take care of everything she might need. Ever."

It was exactly what he'd figured. Jess didn't need the money, but just about the last thing she'd said to Spires before passing out was that she had plans for Mariska. He didn't know how she'd done it, when she would even have had the time, but he wasn't going to tell the CIA about her ill-gotten gains. They'd claimed everything in Fortuna's crypto wallets anyway; the twenty million from the Chechen rebels was a drop in the bucket by comparison.

"You're right," he said, drawing Jess back in for another kiss. "You are perfectly, exactly right."

"Mom!" Mariska yelled from somewhere upstairs. "Mom, can I have this room? The one overlooking the ocean - with the pink bedspread?"

"Of course you can, sweetie!" Jess called back.

"And where am I sleeping?" Pascal asked.

"Oh." She nuzzled her nose against his, her fingers slipping down to undo the top button of his shirt. "I thought you might like to share the master suite."

"I do love the way you think." He sought her mouth for another deep, searing kiss.

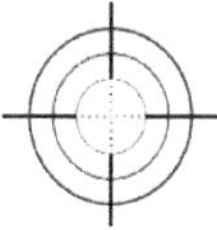

The End

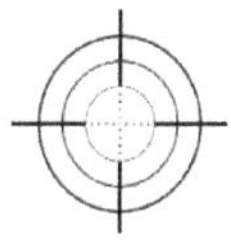

The *Rescue Rangers* will return - and yes, I promise, one day, Mariska will get her own story. ONE DAY. She's just a kid. And now she's got a pair of super-protective parents with some extremely specialized skills looking out for her.

The next book in the *Rescue Rangers* series will be *Ranger's Watch* - where a new recruit to Hestia Global Security finds himself assigned an extremely unlikely target to bodyguard, the ex-wife of one Saul Hayworth, now a country singing sensation. Does the former Mrs Hayworth know anything about what her ex was up to? It's going to be down to Erik Linziger to find out... by any means necessary.

Also By Caitlyn Lynch

RESCUE RANGERS SERIES

RANGER’S RESCUE

RANGER’S HOMECOMING

RANGER'S MISSION

RANGER'S BLOOD

RANGER'S WATCH (forthcoming)

SUNFISH ISLAND RESORT SERIES

FINDING CORY

THE RELUCTANT BILLIONAIRE

HER FAKE ISLAND WEDDING

SLOW SIMMER

FIGHTING FATE

CROP IT LIKE IT'S HOT (In the PICTURES OF YOU anthology)

BETTER IN PRACTICE (UPCOMING)

STANDALONE BOOKS

IF WISHES WERE HORSES - AN IRISH ROMANCE

CAR CRASH LOVE

KITTENS FOR CHRISTMAS

DANA'S DUO

HOT FOR HEATHER

ELEVATOR ENCOUNTERS SERIES

ELLIE'S ENCOUNTER

JULIET'S ROMEO

THE BEST MAN FOR LEAH

RANGER HEAT SERIES

RANGER'S BLOOD

FIRST SUBMISSION

SECOND SURRENDER

THIRD THRILLS

Caitlyn also writes historical romance as Catherine Bilson. You can find her website at catherinebilson.com

www.ingramcontent.com/pod-product-compliance
Lightning Source LLC
Chambersburg PA
CBHW070641310726
48982CB00001B/369
9780645182897